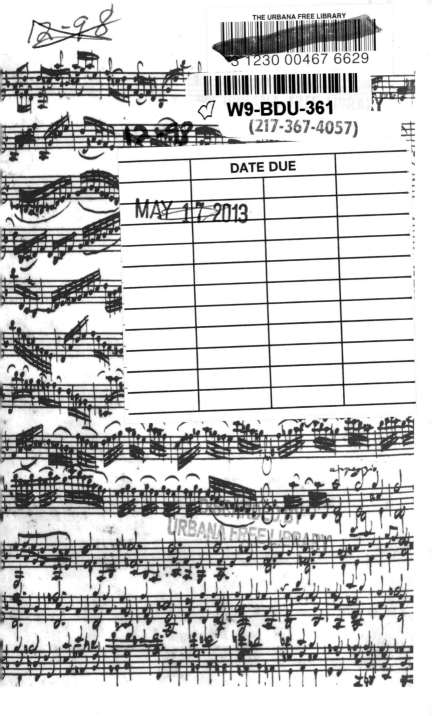

ALSO BY PAOLO MAURENSIG

ᔐ

The Lüneburg Variation

CANONE INVERSO

A NOVEL

PAOLO MAURENSIG

TRANSLATED BY JENNY MCPHEE

HENRY HOLT AND COMPANY

NEW YORK

Henry Holt and Company, Inc.
Publishers since 1866
115 West 18th Street
New York, New York 10011

Henry Holt is a registered trademark of
Henry Holt and Company, Inc.

The translator would like to thank the
Italian Academy for Advanced Studies at
Columbia University for their support and inspiration.

Originally published in Italy in 1996 as *Canone Inverso*
by Arnoldo Mondadori Editore S.p.A., Milano
Published in Canada by Fitzhenry & Whiteside Ltd.
195 Allstate Parkway, Markham, Ontario L3R 4T8

Library of Congress Cataloging-in-Publication Data
Maurensig, Paolo, 1943–
[Canone inverso. English]
Canone inverso : a novel / Paolo Maurensig;
translated by Jenny McPhee.
p.   cm.
ISBN 0-8050-5538-X (hb : alk. paper)
I. McPhee, Jenny.   II. Title.
PQ4873.A8947C3613   1998
853'.914—dc21   98-10774
CIP

First American Edition 1998

Designed by Lucy Albanese

Facsimile of the Chaconne from the D-Major Partita for Solo Violin by Johann
Sebastian Bach, BWV 1004, Staatsbibliothek zu Berlin / Preußischer Kulturbesitz,
Musikabteilung mit Mendelssohn-Archiv

Printed in the United States of America
All first editions are printed on acid-free paper. ∞

1 3 5 7 9 10 8 6 4 2

TO SONIA

CANONE INVERSO

As to the origins of bowed instruments, it is said that the wife of Shiva, the goddess Parvati, felt such great pity for the fate that awaited man at the end of his terrestrial adventure that she decided to give him something that would protect him from demons and help him to find on earth, whenever he wished, the world of the gods. But Shiva, jealous of these attentions, destroyed her gift in one blow. Its fragments fell into the seas and forests, gave life to conchs and tortoises, pressed themselves into the trunks of trees, and even descended into the loins of women. Only the bow fell intact to earth, but it was used for many generations as a weapon. Many divine ages had to pass before man constructed the first lute, using the shell of a turtle. Nevertheless, it was still strummed with the fingers. Only as the most fearsome era drew near did man discover how his bow could be used to vibrate strings, and thereby imitate the eternal sound that began the world—a sigh emanating from the billowing clothes of Shiva, the dancing god, the god who rules the universe and maintains its order.

$\sim$

SOME TIME AGO, at a musical instrument auction at Christie's in London, I bought a violin made by Jakob Stainer, the most highly esteemed seventeenth-century Tyrolean violin maker, for twenty thousand pounds. I considered myself fortunate: I would have paid any price to have it in my possession once more.

The instrument was delivered to me the next morning at the Dorchester Hotel, where I was staying. The accompanying documents stated that the previous owner had been a renowned psychiatric institute in Vienna.

My purchase received, I began a precise and meticulous ritual. First, I ordered lunch in my room. After dismissing the waiter, I locked the door, opened the package, pulled the instrument from the box, and leaned it upright in a low satin armchair I had placed in the center of the room. In order to find the perfect light, I adjusted the blinds and shifted the position of the armchair several times before finally sitting down at the table. I was already anticipating a delicious afternoon—the meeting, the secrecy, the sidelong looks, the expectations: I was behaving just as I had during my first rendezvous with a beautiful woman. The only difference was that the object of my desire was more than three hundred years old. As for the rest, however, it was all there: passion, jealousy, insatiability, all bound to the perpetual fear of loss.

Satisfied with my view of the violin, I prepared to eat my meal in tranquillity. Only when I had finished lunch would I observe my purchase more closely. First, I would feel its weight in my hands for a good long while. Then I would examine every detail with a magnifying glass, including, as far as it was possible, the interior. I had already spied, by peering through one of the sinuous grooves in the shape of an *f,* a faded, barely legible label glued to the back of the violin. I would replace the remaining strings, which were so consumed as to be on the verge of breaking, with a set of new ones. And, finally, I would again listen to her voice.

The instrument was in good condition. Perhaps, over the years, it had not been treated with the utmost care, but the skilled intervention of a violin maker was not necessary, except perhaps to repair some very minor splintering and to retouch the finish here and there. In one place in particular, at the lower end of the instrument, the wood had been rubbed entirely bare: apparently the violin had always been played without a shoulder rest.

One remarkable characteristic of the violin was a tiny anthropomorphic head carved into the top of the pegbox, where one usually finds the traditional scroll. This was an odd characteristic for a violin, because normally these miniature wooden sculptures are found on violas and larger instruments, and most often depict lion heads and grotesque visages whose purpose was not so much ornamental as to ward off evil spirits. This one, instead, was a very precise reproduction of a man's face, perhaps a Mameluke, with a drooping mustache, a ferocious expression, and a wide-open mouth, as if he were screaming in pain or anguish. I had always believed that it was the last violin Stainer ever made, and that, perhaps, he had wanted to depict in that face the insane rage that had overcome him—and eventually killed him.

I had barely sat down at the table when the telephone rang. It was the reception desk announcing the arrival of someone who had come from Christie's. I thought it must concern some additional formality relative to my purchase, but the man who walked into my room some minutes later did not have the demeanor of an employee.

He seemed agitated. He asked me if I was the person who the day before had bought a violin at Christie's. His question was so direct I was afraid that I was in the presence of a police official who was about to inform me that there had been some irregularity about my acquisition. It does in fact happen, albeit rarely, that an object put up for auction has been stolen, lost, or simply not yet approved for sale. If this were the case, the transaction would be nullified. I became very worried. I envisioned myself having to give up my precious violin. But the man, whose name I had already forgotten, was not a representative of the law. The purchase had been entirely regular. He confirmed it so himself as soon as he became aware of my troubled state. He immediately noticed the violin on radiant display in the armchair and, realizing that his intrusion had interrupted my ceremony, wanted to make it up to me in some way. He told me that I had been fortunate not to have come up against other bidders, only paying the initial estimated price for the instrument. He added that though he had known about the auction, due to a series of unfortunate circumstances he had arrived too late for the appointment in the King Street rooms in St. James's. While he was talking, he could not take his eyes from the violin. He circled it, observing it in every possible light. He restrained himself, however, from getting too close, although I could sense his strong desire to examine the violin thoroughly.

I tried to remain firm in my conviction that the stranger did not represent any threat to my precious instrument. I was, however, by no means calm. I was still concerned about the motive for his visit. Judging from his behavior, I would have guessed that he was a collector, a connoisseur of antique instruments, who, having lost his opportunity, had come to congratulate the person who had been more fortunate than he, and to give perhaps a last farewell to that precious object that he had let get away. Unless . . .

That which I had feared happened almost immediately. He became very nervous, as if he were about to make a shady proposition, and he asked me if I would be willing to give him the violin in exchange for double—no, triple—the sum I had paid. Fix any price and I will pay it, he said, nearly swept away by his own pertinacity. Finally, as if exhausted by his outburst, he asked my permission to sit, and let himself fall into an armchair.

"This is the proof that I never dared dream of . . ." I thought I heard him whisper, but the words were evidently not intended for me. Nor did I try to discover what he meant by them. We remained immersed in a silence that seemed endless. I did not feel like asking him anything, and he did not seem disposed to talking. I poured him a glass of wine, which he did not refuse, but he held it in his hand for a long time without lifting it to his lips. He seemed to have calmed himself, or, rather, to have become resigned to the situation. At a certain point, he got up, put down his glass, and, heading toward the door, apologized for the awkward intrusion and for his impossible request. He realized, he said, its callowness. Furthermore, the offer to buy the violin from me at three times the price was unrealistic, as he did not have the money. And in any case, he was certain that even if he did have the money, I would never have agreed to his request. He told me he was very sorry to have disturbed me and to have ruined my lunch.

I felt relieved. But only for a moment. His unexpected decision to leave without telling me who he was and why he was so interested in that violin irritated me.

"Don't you think you owe me an explanation?" I asked him just as he was about to open the door. The man stopped and turned, shaking his head.

"I am not a disappointed collector," he explained, "as my behavior might suggest. Nor am I a violinist," he added. "I am only a dilettante, an amateur. It is true, I own a few instruments, but they do not make up a collection. I have at home a pair of Mittenwald violins, which belonged to my grandfather, and a modern cello, which I sometimes practice upon, but for purely personal pleasure."

"I was convinced you were an expert," I said.

"What little I know about violins I learned from a friend of mine who is a violin maker."

"And why then were you interested in this violin?"

"I am a writer, and this instrument is attached to a story. It is a terrible story, but one that I wish to get to the end of. And the violin is proof that the person who told me the story really existed, even if that doesn't yet explain everything."

" 'Really existed'? What do you mean?" I began to fear that I was in the presence of someone unstable.

In response to this last question the man quickly crossed the room and grabbed the violin with determination. I had not expected the gesture and it frightened me. He carried the instrument over to the window in order to better examine it. "I have your permission, don't I?" I was trembling inside. In that moment he could have done nearly anything: fled out the door with the violin, or, worse, shattered it against the wall, or even, as the window was open, thrown it out onto the crowded Park Lane. Luckily for me, he did not do any of these things, and when he handed me back the violin I felt a sense of contentment, almost joy.

"What did you mean by 'really existed'?" I asked him a second time.

The man thought for a long while before he answered. "I meant really living, in flesh and blood."

He looked at me, studying my reaction. "Please do not think I am insane. I met the owner of this violin, and then later doubted his existence, until I happened by pure chance to be leafing through the Christie's catalog and saw in it his very same instrument. I then felt compelled to own this one piece of proof. But perhaps I should tell you the whole story from the beginning."

I sat down in an armchair, inviting him to do the same and to tell me the story. The stranger hesitated an instant, then began to speak.

THE STORY I am about to tell you took place a year ago in Vienna. As I have said, I am not a musician, only an amateur, a music lover. Music is my consolation. This art, with its elusive essence, with its ability to vanish into thin air, approximates my idea of life.

Last year was the three hundredth anniversary of the birth of Bach, and throughout Europe this date was commemorated by a series of extraordinary concerts. It was a good opportunity to make a musical pilgrimage to various European capitals. One of these stops, after Leipzig and Munich, was naturally Vienna, where the Neue Wiener Barockensemble, directed by Heinz Prammer, was to perform in the Brahmssaal. The program consisted of the six Brandenburg Concertos, the

Suite in C Major, and the Concerto for Violin and Orchestra in E Major, and would take place over two evenings separated by a three-day pause. There was no risk of my becoming bored in the interval, as it was the end of summer, the city was still crowded and festive, and, aside from one or two unexpected storms, the weather was fair.

On the night before the second concert, I ate, as usual, in a restaurant on the Operngasse. It was still early when I finished, and as I had no intention of returning home to sleep, I hailed a taxi and asked to be taken to Grinzing, the famous district known for its *Heurigen,* taverns where one drinks delicious wine. I strolled along the streets of the quarter, peering through windows and into courtyards in search of a welcoming but not too crowded place in which to spend the rest of the evening. I stopped before a sign depicting a detail from a painting by Brueghel the Elder: peasants dancing to the music of a reed pipe. The image was surrounded by the words "love," "friendship," and "music." And judging from the music flowing into the street, the place did seem to offer, if not love and friendship, at least a little joy. Inside there were quite a lot of people, but I managed to find myself a table.

THE VIENNESE in Vienna, particularly in the summer, are a small minority among legions of tourists. Yet that evening, in that tavern, I was convinced I was one of the few foreigners present, if not, indeed, the only one. Around me everyone was drinking, talking. Every so often there would be a toast, which despite my usual reserve I joined in making. The buzzing of the voices was dense but contained in such a way as not to disturb those who preferred listening to the music. On a wooden platform two musicians, one playing a guitar, the other a zither, performed popular tunes. It didn't occur to anyone to sing along (a common practice in beer halls), but at the end of each song there were generous applause and additional toasts.

For a long time I had been thinking of writing a story with music as the protagonist. It is well known that music can give great emphasis to a poetic or theatrical text, rendering verses sublime that would otherwise be rather banal. I, on the contrary, found it quite difficult to make music evoke or suggest something dramatic. In fact, music for me had always been a safe refuge from the dramas of life. And yet in that moment an annoying idea was insinuating itself into my thoughts. Music elevates the feelings and the very nature of man, but in order to reach such heights he must pass through a good deal of screeching, roaring, and dissonance. Behind the refined music we hear performed with levity and perfection by an orchestra or a string quartet, there is the straining of nerves, the gushing of blood, the breaking of hearts. I was suddenly alarmed by the thought of my beloved art in this different light. I imagined the infinity of sounds rising night and day throughout the world, and I thought of the efforts of the many individuals scattered across the earth, fighting continuously in order to keep music alive, like an army that keeps moving despite the devastation of enemy fire, replacing its losses with ever-new forces and sowing in its stead a battlefield of the dead.

I was mulling over this thought while observing the two musicians, who, having exhausted their repertoire and scraped up a few schillings to pay for tomorrow's meal, were preparing to leave. They looked very much alike: they were old men, perhaps brothers, and wore clothes that were too heavy for the season. Even their movements, as they collected the scores from their music stands or placed their instruments back in their cases, were similar. In a series of gestures that they obviously had repeated for who knows how many years, they slung their cases over their shoulders, put their hats on their heads, and then slowly drained the glasses of wine someone had offered them at the end of the evening. I hadn't realized it, but one of the two, the one who played the zither, was blind, and as he walked he rested a hand on his companion's shoulder.

As I watched them leave, I was overcome by melancholy. Perhaps this was their only means of earning a living. And I wondered if it was only chance or if there was some behind-the-scenes manager who arranged where and when they played. As if to fill the void they had left, the conversation at the tables suddenly picked up, but without the background of music all joy was lost, and it seemed there was nothing left in the world to which one could make a toast.

A little while later the door to the tavern opened, causing the cluster of tiny bells hanging above the doorjamb to jingle. And in he came, the man who is the subject of this story.

HIS AGE was indeterminable and he was dressed as a coachman, wearing boots, an oilskin cloak, and a derby. His unexpected appearance put an end to all conversation. It was unclear who he was, whether a beggar or a thief. From the back of the room came a few giggles, which were almost immediately extinguished. We all remained silent until, having reached the platform, the man bowed several times toward the public and, doffing his hat with a clownlike haughtiness, proclaimed, in all seriousness, that we should consider ourselves fortunate to have the opportunity to hear, "for a sum that only your good hearts can determine," a great violinist. With these words the entire room came back to life. Someone in the back shouted something at him, and he retorted with a phrase in a dialect I did not understand, but to which many responded with applause.

The man had a considerable mustache, gray and drooping like a Tartar's. His hair, by contrast, was still dark, and long enough to be gathered into a ponytail held by an elastic band. On closer observation, I still found it difficult to determine his age, although he was certainly well beyond fifty. His face was like a mask: ruddy, with wild eyes, and the expressions of a mime. His voice was sonorous, his gestures eloquent. He could have been a minstrel who had fallen off a caravan from another era.

After removing his cloak, which revealed a threadbare striped shirt covered by a pair of garish red suspenders, he opened a shabby cardboard case, and extracting a violin, he lifted it to his shoulder and tuned the strings. From the audience there immediately arose a chorus of requests, which the man, after a little while, began to fulfill: Strauss, Lehár, *The Csárdás Princess*, and "The Blue Danube." He played everything with mastery and a torrent of variations that sent the listeners into raptures. After a while, he came down off the platform and moved among the tables, improvising, according to whom he found before him, the part of cupid with lovers, or the part of a seducer with lonely women. He did not hesitate to play jokes on the audience. He went as close as possible to couples, especially those who had a certain clandestine air about them, and if the man seemed reluctant to give him money, he would elbow him in the chest as he tickled the décolletage of the young woman with the tip of his bow, all the while continuing to play. Even if sometimes he went too far, no one seemed to take offense. He enjoyed the same impunity as an actor who plays the role of a villain. Even his clothes, obviously washed only by the rain, seemed an elaborate costume. In very little time, he established not only trust, but complicity with his public.

The table where I was sitting was far from his improvised stage, but he winked in my direction often, as if he wanted to reassure our side of the room that we hadn't been forgotten and that soon he would come over to us. I wondered with what spirit I would endure his shenanigans, if he did, in fact, approach me.

In the meantime, the violinist put on a good show, and his audience responded with rounds of applause that filled him with renewed energy. Besides Strauss's waltzes and light-opera arias, he performed highly complicated Hungarian Gypsy pieces, in which he not only displayed enormous talent, but acrobatic skills as well. He could hold his violin in the most unthinkable positions. In between one piece and the next, he paused to drink the wine offered him by exuberant spectators. Every so often, he made a round of the tables and his hat filled with coins and bills. Full as it was, he replaced the hat on his head and continued to play with fresh enthusiasm. But when, a little while later, he removed the hat again, it was clean empty. His little trick caused everyone to erupt in hysterical laughter, earning him more applause, and more money, which also disappeared into his magician's hat.

Watching him, I returned to my reflections. Here was a superb example of one of music's fighters, or, better yet, of a lost soldier, and I tried to imagine him as a child before a music stand, intent on extracting notes from his unobliging instrument. I imagined the years of study, the aspirations, the first steps into the world of music, and finally a career, who knows for what reason, interrupted. But had he really been a professional musician? I was not entirely convinced. During concerts I often observed the ranks of the orchestra, and in particular the string section, and I always noted how neat and disciplined the musicians were, like scribes or copyists, true and proper calligraphers of music, sacrificed to a rigorous, pedantic, and meticulous job. As is true of many other professions, a violinist's job entails physical stresses that over time become unequivocally etched onto the person's physiognomy. A violinist who plays in an orchestra is marked by the instrument that has lorded over him for a lifetime. And with age, the traces of this servitude become increasingly evident: his eyes possess a kind of moodiness, and his gestures reveal his absolute dedication. The orchestral violinist does not possess the tenacity of the soloist who wants to bend the notes to his will. Instead, music for him is simply material: sounds with different pitches and durations to be reproduced with precision. The sacred fire no longer burns within him, but smolders in quiet remission. Only the youngest, who are at the beginning of their careers and have yet to endure visible deformations, continue for a while to *make music*, without resting their heads on their violins as if on pillows. And though their efforts are at times modest and the score does not rise to great heights, still they play as if the success of the entire concert depended solely on the notes coming from their instruments.

The violinist before me, though advanced in years, was somehow immune to these characteristics. In fact, he behaved as if his role had always been only that of a soloist. At the same time, however, he treated his violin, and the music itself, with insolence, and his attitude while playing bordered on contempt. I wondered what could have possibly happened to him in his life that caused him to place his instrument and his art at the mercy of a tavern audience.

Once again, he descended from the platform with the violin under his arm. He calmly drank another glass of wine, and then, strumming the instrument's soundboard with his fingers, he made it roll like a drum. When the room became silent, he declared with the gravity of a circus barker announcing a show never before seen on earth that he would put his violin at the service of the highest bidder. Whoever paid the right sum—a sum that was, of course, negotiable—would be able to listen to any piece of music, even the most difficult, he desired. Requests immediately arose, which he summarily rejected with a wave of his hand, as if to say: "Much too easy! I need a far greater challenge!" He moved from table to table, and every so often appeared to wink in my direction. He looked at me, but he didn't come near me. I deduced that like a delicious morsel I was being kept for last. And in fact, after making a large circle around the tables, he stopped in front of mine. He had guessed, I don't know how, that I was a foreigner (only later did I realize that the program for the Bach concerts was sticking out of my jacket pocket), and exclaimed in a loud voice: "Oh, look what we have here! A fellow who has actually come to Vienna just to hear good music." The room again became silent, and the violinist expertly took advantage of this pause, delaying with felicitous effect his punch line. "What would such a gentleman wish to hear?" he said finally.

Annoyed by his facile mockery, I tried to respond in kind. "And you, sir, what would it please you to play?"

"That which the gentleman would like to hear."

"Anything at all I wish?"

"Anything!"

At that point, I no longer had any hesitations.

"I would gladly listen to Bach's Chaconne."

And with this I believed I had protected myself from all further provocation. But I was wrong. The man remained planted before me in all his arrogance. He raised his arm in order to quiet the audience, which was watching the scene with amusement.

"Here finally," he said, "we have a connoisseur. Someone who truly knows how to appreciate good music. He deserves a toast." He motioned to the waitress, who after bringing him a glass, quickly slipped away, barely escaping his clutches. Against my wishes, I accepted his invitation to stand and toast with him. He drank down his wine in one gulp, smoothed his mustache beaded with golden drops, and with the back of his hand rubbed his nose as if he had smelled a good deal. After burping solemnly, he asked me:

"And how much would you be willing to pay to hear this Chaconne?"

Now, the Chaconne, as you know, is a piece as beautiful as it is difficult. And I suddenly thought I knew what he was up to: whatever amount I proposed, he would claim was too little, and with that or another excuse he would move on. I am not a poker player, but I cannot resist calling a bluff. So I made an offer that I was sure he could not refuse.

"Would a thousand schillings be enough?"

In comparison with the change he had collected so far that night, a thousand schillings was a jackpot.

"A thousand schillings," the man repeated. "A thousand schillings!" he shouted at the room, and his expression, which up until then had been a clown's cheerful mask, in an instant became sad, as if he had been gravely offended and couldn't defend himself. He turned his back to me and moved slowly away, his shoulder blades pointed and sticking out of his tight and filthy shirt. My assessment had been correct! He was fleeing. I should have felt vindicated, but I hadn't really wanted to win that hand. I watched him go, his feet shuffling, his body hunching over. He rested his cheek on his violin, as if he were listening to its heart, taking its weak pulse. At that moment I would have liked to have called him back and apologized for my offense. But while he slowly made his way to the platform, the room already resounded with the first moving chords of the Chaconne.

I HAVE OFTEN wondered how long it takes for the last note of a piece of music to be completely extinguished: not only physically, as a sound vibration, but as an emotional vibration.

It seemed to me that no one dared to applaud, that the music itself had removed all will. It was a moment in which the world had stopped on its axis and was having trouble putting itself back into motion. Certainly, the interval of time that occurred between the last note of the violinist's impeccable performance and the first clap of hands (mine), which then immediately multiplied into passionate applause, seemed to last an eternity.

Now, however, there was a bill to pay. The other customers cast sidelong glances in my direction in order to glean my state of mind. But that individual, for whom I won't deny I was feeling great admiration, enjoyed the moment of his victory with great calm. He ordered another glass of wine (the number of glasses he had drunk over the course of the evening was by now uncountable), he rubbed his mustache with the sleeve of his shirt, and, finally, leaning his violin against his coat, which was draped over a chair, he came toward me with his hat in hand, like a beggar. Everyone wanted to see if I would truly honor my debt. But the thousand-schilling banknote that I placed in his hat was folded in such a way that only he could see it.

"Many thanks, sir," he said, with a smile that clearly implied confrontation. "I am forever at your service, sir," he murmured through his teeth, and balancing his hat on the palm of his hand, he raised his middle finger in an obscene gesture that only I could see.

AWAKENED BY the sound of an insistent hammer, I found myself back in my hotel room. I opened my eyes, and at the thought of what had happened the previous night, at the memory of that man's mocking face, I felt a burning sense of defeat. In addition, I had a headache. And there is nothing worse than feeling frustrated while also suffering from a hangover.

I wondered how I had made it back to the hotel. All I could remember was the violinist's offensive gesture. It was as if whatever had happened next had been canceled from my memory. Then, with difficulty, I began to recall.

Having pocketed my banknote, the man had turned his back to me and faced the audience, which loudly urged him: "Maestro, play something merry for us!" I remained in my seat, wearing a hardened smile, as if I had a bone between my teeth. I hoped no one had seen anything. I was tired and wanted to leave, but I wasn't sure what to do. To go at that point was comparable to desertion. And I was certain that man would never let me leave without a biting farewell comment. I had to wait until the right moment. So I ordered another drink. I was, however, exceeding my limits: I am someone who can normally hold his wine, but my legs were already feeling wobbly, and I wasn't convinced that I would be able to walk quickly. I paid the bill and was ready to make my move. The way out, fortunately, was not far away. I had only to seize the moment in which "my friend" was occupied enough so as not to become aware of my flight. When I saw that he was entirely absorbed in *A Waltz Dream*, I got up and took my first steps toward the door. But I moved too slowly and didn't succeed in reaching the door in time. The violinist abruptly stopped playing. I turned and saw him collapse in the middle of the tables with a great crash, overturning chairs and shattering glasses. In the confusion that followed, I managed to make it to the door and leave the tavern, but once in the street my legs started to fail me. I began to wander, zigzagging my way through the quarter. The streets were still crowded, but by now all the taverns and restaurants were closed, and appeared as ships that had already weighed anchor. I, alone and too late, had been abandoned on the pier. After that, all I could remember were the approaching lights of an automobile, perhaps a taxi, with people inside singing cheerfully, who had the kindness to invite me into their chorus and take me back to my hotel.

I MUST HAVE slept a long time. It wasn't dawn, as I had believed when I first awoke, but after midday, and that distant hammering sound was nothing other than the knock of the maid who had come to make up my room. By raising my hoarse voice, I managed to chase off this zealous annoyance with the excuse that I was not feeling well.

I did not get out of bed until late in the afternoon. I ordered a cup of strong coffee, and after soaking for a long while in a hot tub, I convinced myself that I was once again presentable to the outside world. I went out. The air and the magnetism of the crowd reinvigorated me. I felt completely recovered. And my appetite had returned, so I stopped at a food stall to have a bite to eat.

That night at the Brahmssaal the program consisted of the second part of the Brandenburg Concertos. Up until the day before, I would have said that nothing in the world could have kept me from going to that concert. After all, I had come to Vienna for that purpose alone.

Though it was early, I hailed a taxi, got in, and settled myself comfortably, but instead of telling the driver to take me to the Brahmssaal, I heard myself say "Grinzing." I still had unfinished business in the tavern of the previous night that I considered so necessary and urgent that it needed to be taken care of that very evening. Besides, it was early, and there was still enough time to make the concert. But first I felt compelled to see that bizarre character again, or at least find out something about him. A man like that could not pass unobserved: I would surely find someone who could tell me who he was. Having arrived at my destination, I paid the taxi driver and began walking in search of the tavern where I had encountered the violinist. It was seven o'clock on an August evening, the sun still had not set, and in the fading daylight the district appeared empty and lifeless. The *Heurigen* would only begin to get crowded around ten o'clock.

It was not long before I came across the sign for the tavern. I went inside, but the place did not seem the same. I tried to locate where I had been sitting the night before, but the tables and chairs were now arranged in a way that was entirely different. On the wooden platform, which had been moved into a corner, a lone acoustic guitar player was adjusting the speakers and practicing a song or two from his repertoire on a single family of tourists.

A waitress entered the room. I thought I recognized her as the girl who had served me the night before, and I asked her about the violinist. She looked at me with surprise; she didn't know any violinist. She explained that itinerant musicians came into the place continually. The taverns did not hire them; they were simply given a space where they could play, as long as they didn't annoy the customers. And it was very rare for one of them to return to the same place several evenings in a row. Sometimes they would come back after a few months; other times they would disappear altogether. She had no idea where they went, and perhaps no one knew.

I felt the need to persist. It was impossible, I said, that she didn't remember that man, seeing as it was only the evening before that she had repeatedly served him drinks.

At these words the girl widened her eyes: "Last night? Oh, but last night was my night off," she said. "The girl you saw was my sister. But she isn't working again until tomorrow. Wait a minute while I go ask around for you." She came back after a few minutes with the owner, to whom I had to explain everything all over again. He, too, said he didn't know of any strange or bizarre violinist, that there were so many musicians that went around the taverns in the evening that it was impossible to keep track. They come and go, he said, as if he were talking about trains, and who could possibly remember them all?

I remarked that he should remember the violinist of the previous evening since he had fallen to the ground and created something of a ruckus. At these words, the owner smiled and with cold humor objected that in Grinzing no one got too worried if, after a certain hour at night, someone was not able to stand on his legs.

When I left, I was not at all convinced. I put my head into a few other taverns, asked the same questions, but everywhere was given the same evasive response. I began to believe that they had mistaken me for an inspector from the department of labor.

I left Grinzing rather irritated, and in a taxi I went to the Brahmssaal. I knew that by now I was late, but I wanted to prove to myself that I had intended to go. When I arrived, the concert had indeed already begun. After the intermission, I found my seat and listened to, or at least thought I did, the second half of the concert. Then, when it was over, I took another taxi to the Kärtnerstrasse, and from there I walked toward Saint Stephen's Cathedral.

For a little while I let myself be carried by the crowd. At every street corner, at every open space, I came across musicians, mostly young, who played their instruments and relied on the generosity of passersby. But, as if suspended from a thread above the hubbub of the city, I kept hearing notes from a violin, that same violin. Sometimes the sound moved off into the distance, sometimes it was altogether silent. Then I would hear it again, farther away this time, as if it wanted to flee from me but at the same time guide me.

That sound, I well realized, existed only in my excited imagination, and yet the illusion was perfect. Even the wind, which had suddenly come up, confused my senses with its whisper. The notes I thought had vanished were all of a sudden very close to me, only to be transformed into the creak of a shutter or the tinkle of a tin sign.

Enchanted by that imaginary music, I separated myself from the flow of the crowd and walked in the direction of the Danube. After passing through dark streets and across squares and parks, I sat down exhausted at an outdoor table in the courtyard of a restaurant. Since the sky was cloudy and the wind had picked up, the other customers had all retreated inside. The waitress invited me to do the same, but I preferred to stay outside. A minute or so later, a few raindrops plopped into my beer mug and spread themselves over the red checked tablecloth. But the much-feared downpour never arrived. Nevertheless, no one returned outdoors. So I remained alone in the deserted courtyard. Since I was too tired to continue walking, I decided to enjoy the recently cooled air for a moment.

I had already finished my beer and was considering ordering another when I heard footsteps behind me.

At a certain point they stopped. I waited for the person to begin walking again and head past me toward the entrance to the restaurant. But he didn't move. I turned my head a little and saw out of the corner of my eye a motionless shape a few meters away. When he spoke, I instantly recognized the voice.

"So tonight we have renounced good music for some typical local folklore?"

I jolted around and there he was, wearing his dark overcoat, his derby pressed down on his head, and his violin resting on his shoulder. If the devil had appeared before me, I would not have been more surprised.

The man snickered. "May I sit down?" And without waiting for a nod from me, he put down his cardboard case, wrapped twice around with string, on the table, tossed his oilcloth cape back behind his shoulders, sat down across from me, and waved over the waitress, who in that moment had appeared at the door. He ordered a brandy and a beer. And my empty mug was soon brimming over with fresh foam.

Although disturbing, the coincidence seemed extraordinary to me. Two people in a city of three million meeting at an odd hour and in an out-of-the-way place, where neither of the two should have reasonably been, subverted every sane principle of chance. Who knows what constellations combined to cause that imaginary music to make its way into my mind?

While taking off his hat in order to put it down on the table, a coin fell out of the brim and rolled onto the tablecloth.

"I thought I might go inside here," said the man, "to get out of the rain, and maybe earn a bit of change. But today my friend will not hear of it."

As he said this, he untied the case and slipped the violin inside, handling it proudly. I had already noticed the night before that it was a special instrument. I had thought immediately that it was a Stainer, or in any case a Tyrolean violin. I had been struck by the small head that was in the place of the traditional scroll. And now I could see that cruel and threatening face up close. I noticed right away that there was something of a resemblance to the man sitting across from me, as if he had, over time, purposefully altered his features to look like the face on his violin. How such an instrument had found its way into the hands of a vagabond was a mystery—a mystery I wanted to solve.

He stared tenderly and for a long time at his violin. Then, finally, he closed the case and tied it again with great care.

"In any case," he went on, "today I can allow myself a vacation." And with the gesture of a magician, between his fingers appeared the thousand-schilling banknote. "I can also allow myself to buy you a drink," he added, as he indicated to the waitress that he wanted to order another round.

"A vacation that you have more than earned," I said obligingly. I no longer felt any resentment toward him. The violinist's face was not as I remembered it. Without his clownish expression, and far from the scene of his performance, he was just a lonely, vulnerable man weighed down by the years.

"It takes a great talent to play that piece," I added. The man remained silent, as if he were considering what I had said. Then he corrected me:

"In order to play that piece, great technical skills are needed. And technique sometimes disguises itself as talent. Oh, the difference is minimal, imperceptible to the listener. But not to the player. I do not mean that talent does not require effort. That would be impossible. To reach perfection, technique, practice, and dedication are all necessary."

After a silence during which he seemed to have guessed my thoughts, he continued: "How in the world, you are asking yourself, did a man who can play the violin with such skill end up as an itinerant musician in taverns and restaurants? A legitimate question. And the response is simple: ambition. Because of the overwhelming and destructive desire to reach perfection. But what is perfection? It is the vanishing point at the end of an endless road, it is the mirage that continuously moves out of our reach, it is the last rung of a circular ladder.

"Perfection, you see, is related to infinity, but infinity is not only the infinitely big. It is also the infinitely small. Perfection can suggest the idea of forward movement, but also the idea of coming to a halt. The search for perfection proceeds with a pace that becomes infinitely slower. It is a continuous progression that nevertheless gradually reduces itself as it approaches its goal.

"When I was a child, I remember buying a marble from a junk dealer for five cents, but I realized soon afterwards that other dealers were selling the same marble for only four cents. So I returned immediately to the dealer who had sold it to me, demanding that he give me back the one penny extra I had paid, but he would not hear of it: It was his right to establish the price of the goods he sold. I left feeling very angry with him and with myself for having let myself be cheated. On my way home, I thought of how I could repair the damage caused by my hasty decision. And I realized that if I had bought another identical marble for four cents, my loss would be halved, and buying yet another, it would be reduced by a third, and another by a fourth, and so on. But even if I persisted in buying for all of eternity an infinite number of marbles, my loss would continue to divide but would never be eliminated. And yet the goal, in this case, was apparently reachable, the way there deceptively brief."

"Don't you think," I said, "you are exaggerating just a little? After all, what we're talking about is simply playing an instrument well."

By the way he glared at me I understood that the man did not like to be contradicted. "In order to make this statement with such confidence, you yourself must be a musician? You play an instrument?"

"Only for pure personal pleasure. I am actually a writer."

"Ah," said the man, and for a moment it seemed that all of his attention was focused on me. "A writer? What do you write?"

"Just stories."

"And I bet you have written who-knows-how-many stories about music?"

It was a question I had been asked many times.

"I wish it were so," I responded with a slight tremor in my voice, as if I needed to justify myself for an unpardonable omission. "Unfortunately, music has not succeeded in inspiring me to write a story about it. And I am unable to make it descend to the level of human endeavors, as I am able to do with, for example, love, money, and power. So there you have it." And then, to get myself out of a conversation that I found embarrassing, I exclaimed, "But then isn't music, perhaps, a way of overcoming all of these things?"

"Overcoming?" The man looked at me incredulously.

"Yes," I said, trying to sound convinced, "overcoming."

"Overcoming . . ." Judging from the bitter tone of voice he used, the word evoked in him something unpleasant. "You speak as a listener, not as a player. Surely that instrument you play for pleasure—"

"A cello," I quickly specified.

"Surely the cello that you play for purely personal pleasure was imposed upon you by a father and mother who had ambitions for you or who were themselves music lovers. You are of an age, it seems to me, that would make it reasonable to assume that during your childhood you were subjected to the not wholly contemptible habit of music lessons."

"This is true."

"And naturally the hours you passed extracting

notes from your cello were a torment. As a child you were forced to make music. You couldn't refuse. But, in retrospect, you feel obligated to show gratitude toward your father and mother for having made you, against your wishes, practice the cello. Music is now part of your cultural patrimony. You can appreciate it, talk about it with competence, and even play it if you wish. Am I right?"

I had to admit he was.

"Here you are wrong."

"I don't understand."

"Music is not that!" the violinist protested. "The true musician is a descendant of Cain." Then, almost as if he regretted the brusque way he had spoken to me, he was silent for a long time. He shook his head at my incapacity to understand, while searching deep inside himself for words and ideas. His eyes were near closed in an effort to remember something, and his face, with its guard down, was exposed in all its devastation. Finally, he came back to himself and turned to me with his intense expression that suggested a drunk or a clown.

"Since you are a writer, maybe you have heard the popular Hungarian fairy tale that tells the story of a violinist who plays with such passion that one day his soul leaves him and inhabits his violin. From that day on, the violinist can never leave his violin, and he is forced to play the instrument without rest, because only when he plays does he feel alive. . . ." The man interrupted himself as if suddenly struck by the doubt that the metaphor he had chosen did not adequately express his idea. He then tried another approach. "You have probably never worried about certain bodily functions such as respiration, digestion, or your heartbeat. Lungs, heart, intestines work for you regardless of your awareness or wishes, something you only realize when those organs stop functioning normally.

"But let's consider a case in which suddenly, in order to stay alive, you were forced to regulate these organs consciously, using your will. Imagine having to make your heart beat by commanding it to do so, or your lungs breathe, or having to regulate your blood pressure yourself, or the replacement of cells, or the elimination of the thousands of poisons you ingest every day. And to do all of this with the knowledge that one mistake, or even a moment of distraction, would be fatal to you. Can you imagine this?"

Of course I could imagine it. But I couldn't understand what he meant by it.

"Try to imagine being obligated to defeat death moment by moment, maintaining a continuous struggle, a vigilance that keeps you awake night and day.

This effort, however, shouldn't affect the rest of your daily life—your emotions, your duties, your everyday habits. To the eyes of others, not even the shadow of your anxiety should be perceptible; everything should go along with the greatest possible levity, with supreme naturalness, without letting anyone see your extreme concentration.

"Now, try to substantiate the conventional idea that you have of music, give it bones and nerves, blood and sperm, imprison it in a body, in a brain, imagine music as a person, who, in order not to die, must concentrate without respite on the sound of his violin, on the movement of a bow that bounces and rubs across the strings, eliciting chords, melodies, rhythms. Imagine that this was his only possibility of surviving, because silence would cause life itself to dissolve."

"Better to die, then!" I exclaimed, disconcerted. "What could possibly attract us to such an existence?"

The man sneered with pleasure, as if he had been waiting for this reaction. "But it is obvious," he said. "Music! Our very torment would also be the only reason to live."

I didn't know what to say. I realized that this man, by the force of his talk, was manipulating me, dragging me with him, I didn't know where.

"For you to understand what music is and where

this tremendous passion can lead, I must tell you from the beginning the story of that violinist whose soul was imprisoned in his violin. But first there is another story, which I have never told anyone. I don't believe I have much time left, but before I return to where I came from, I would like to tell my story to you. One day you might write it down for me."

The waitress reappeared and the violinist ordered another round. We were still alone sitting beneath the wisteria at an outdoor table. Voices and laughter continued to emanate from inside the restaurant. Every so often, drafts of pungent humidity came off the river, carrying the vague, sweetish odor of decomposing grass. In the street a lone pedestrian whistled in vain for his dog lost among the flowerbeds of a public park. Like lace, the tops of buildings jutted into the sky, and here and there a light in a window perforated their gray facades. The last clouds retreated like the rear guard of a defeated army. And I was a writer in search of a story.

THE MAN BEGAN his story in a peculiar manner:

That which I am about to tell you here in Vienna on the twenty-eighth of August, 1985, is the inviolable truth.

My name is Jenö Varga and I was born in Nagyret, a town in Hungary near the Slovenian and Austrian borders. I am illegitimate, a bastard. I never knew my father's name, even if later in life I believed I had come close to discovering his identity. My mother, when I began to ask her the first embarrassing questions, told me that my father had died during the Great War. But privately she held out the hope that one day he would return. She spoke about him often to me. She never tried to avoid the subject. In fact, she wanted me to be fully aware of my situation. When I was about four years old, she described my father to me as a brave hero in a handsome uniform riding on horseback. As a child, I sat for hours and hours on the front steps of the house watching the road and imagined seeing him arrive with a busby placed firmly on his head, a cloak draped over his shoulders, riding a skittish bay horse whose hooves sent sparks flying from the cobblestones. I thought so much about his homecoming that sometimes at night, even the distant sound of a horse stamping his hoof on the road was enough to wake me and send me running to the window. When someone asked me where my father was, I did not respond—as did many of my peers about their fathers—that he had died during the war (at that stage in life, I could not fathom the concept of death), but claimed instead that he would return on a galloping horse with his saber drawn for all to see. In pronouncing these words, my conviction was so great my playmates believed I spoke the truth.

My mother had kept only two items belonging to my father: a gold locket she never removed from around her neck, and *this* violin, to which my life's destiny became tied. At the time, the instrument was locked in a wooden case. I remember that when my mother showed it to me for the first time, I didn't dare to touch it. Even then musical instruments excited in me an irresistible attraction, and above all the violin, for which I had always harbored the compound feeling of both love and fear. Naturally, I was very impressed by the sculpted face at the top of the pegbox, which to me appeared alive and on the verge of speaking. I could only relax when my mother had put the instrument back in its case, locked it, and replaced the key on top of the chest of drawers in the bedroom. For some time the violin's presence disturbed my sleep, especially when my mother sent me to bed alone. But then, once I discovered where the key to that miniature trunk was hidden, many times curiosity got the better of my fear and I lifted the lid. A shiver would run through my body from head to toe when, with the same caution that I would have used to caress a sleeping tiger, I passed a hand over those taut strings. I had come to believe that violins were living creatures, who with a mere scratch from a stick of wood would awaken and begin to sing.

In my village, only at weddings and country fairs did one have the opportunity to meet violinists. Still, I was bewitched by that sound. I remember that at the annual village festival, there once a caravan of Gypsies who sold horses and copper goods. One morning, I was wandering among the various stands with my mother when I heard the sound of Gypsy music very close by, and I followed it. Almost without wanting to, I found myself going in the direction of their camp. When I was near enough, I squatted down and listened. I don't know for how long I had been there when one of the violinists, alerted by a barking dog, became aware of my presence and started moving toward me, all the while continuing to play and staring me straight in the eye as if he wanted to hypnotize me. I knew very well what they said about Gypsies: they kidnapped children in order to sell them as slaves or, after mutilating them, send them out to beg. And yet, though my legs were desperate to flee as the man approached, I couldn't move. My fascination with his music was stronger than my fear. I don't know what would have happened if my mother hadn't suddenly appeared at the last minute.

MY GRANDPARENTS DIED of Spanish fever when I was only a few months old. My mother, alone and without money, was forced to take the most humiliating jobs. Finally, she found employment in a slaughterhouse, where, together with other women, she ground meat for sausages and salamis. But she was still young and beautiful, and soon the owner, a stout man much older than she, fell in love with her. He relieved her from that thankless job and promoted her to the labeling and packaging department; and when she began to keep the books, respond to the company correspondence, and take care of clients, she became his faithful and irreplaceable assistant. He then started to take her out and even visit her at home. He brought her flowers and other presents, and finally asked her to marry him.

My mother, perhaps thinking of my future, accepted. We moved out of our house in order to go live on my stepfather's farm. We were surrounded by pigsties spread out across a field of mud, from which emanated on certain days an intolerable odor that insinuated itself into the house, permeating everything. My stepfather almost never took off his blood-and-mud-stained apron. And I found that I had as a father, instead of a courageous cavalryman, a nouveau-riche pork butcher, a man that I respected even if I never was able to feel affection for him, though his nature was jovial and kind, and we never wanted for anything.

In the period after the war, as his company became increasingly prosperous, my stepfather took off the filthy apron and put on a dark suit and many gold chains. He often was obliged to take long trips which kept him away from home for weeks at a time.

It was after returning from one of these business trips that he gave me a violin. It was actually my mother who had suggested it to him, but I was grateful to him anyway. It was a miniature instrument, a fourth the size of a regular violin, because I was only seven years old. And when I held it in my arms for the first time, tickling the strings with the bow, I felt as if there were a hand resting on mine and guiding it. Almost without realizing it, I picked out the notes of a song my mother used to sing. Only a few notes, but they filled me with a joy I had never felt before in my life. My mother was visibly moved, perhaps because in that moment she was thinking of the past. And my stepfather, proud of himself and his gift, jokingly predicted a future of greatness for me.

I WAS CONVINCED that my real father would have been the best possible teacher. My stepfather, unfortunately, was more concerned with cold cuts than music. So, for a few years, I played the violin as if it were a game. Without anyone teaching me, I learned how to tune it and to play all the songs I knew, with many variations and diminutions. If someone sang a new motif in my presence, I was capable of reproducing it immediately. And I was also able to improvise my own melodies. I didn't, however, know how to read music, and was utterly unaware of music theory, excepting what little I was learning at school during the singing hour.

One day my elementary-school teacher came to our house to talk to my mother. He had overheard my playing and said he thought it would be a terrible shame if this talent of mine wasn't encouraged. Of course, in the village there was no music school, but he knew a violinist who had played for many years in the Budapest State Orchestra who could teach me, at least initially. If my mother agreed, he would go himself to discuss the matter with him. My mother agreed on the one condition that my academic studies did not suffer. As for myself, I solemnly gave my consent, though I was excited and could not wait to get started. I was thrilled by the thought of learning something new on my beloved instrument. And I wasn't at all worried by the fact that this teacher lived rather far away, some twenty kilometers that I would have to walk once a week. There were many farmers' carts on that road, and someone would surely give me a ride.

The man who was to teach me the art of the violin was rather old and had a surly disposition. He lived alone in a house abandoned to disorder. The only visible violin was hanging from a wire on the wall. From the dust that had accumulated on its bridge, it was obvious that no one had touched it in a long time.

My first audition was the most humiliating experience of my life. I was sure that my talent was going to astound my teacher. Instead, this man interrupted me after only a few notes. He walked over to me with a scandalized expression on his face and tore the violin out of my hands. He then pushed my head to one side, straightened my back, and lifted my elbow with such abrupt and exaggerated movements that I was in pain. It was as if he were trying to stuff me alive into a suit several sizes too small. Only after he had "shaped" me into a position that I considered grotesque did he return my violin, warning me not to move from that stance. If it was too difficult to play, so be it, but he made it clear that it would be curtains for me if I dared to move even a millimeter! That day and on all the following days, during the hour of the lesson he did absolutely everything except listen to my music. He did not even concern himself with checking on me. He would turn his back to me and read or write or stare out the window, utterly absorbed in his thoughts. Sometimes I had the impression that if I stopped playing and tiptoed out of the room, he would not have noticed. But, in fact, he was observing me as if he had eyes in the back of his head, because now and again he instructed me to raise my elbow or straighten my back precisely at the moment, I must admit, when I was beginning to let them fall. His sole concern was to raise me in service of the instrument. He treated me like one of those plants that have to be tied to a stake so that as they grow their form becomes beautiful but unnatural. The violin was being grafted onto me in order for it to take root. I too had to merge with it and feel my veins and my nerves infuse its hard wood. For one year I went to my weekly lesson and not once did we speak of music, but only of how to mold the body to music.

Have you ever thought about how unnatural a violinist's position is? Imagine removing the instrument from his hands while he is playing and looking at him. Don't those stiff limbs, those half-closed eyes, that pronated left forearm, and the tilted head remind you of the deposition from the Cross?

MY STEPFATHER'S BUSINESS was doing better and better, and after a few years we moved to Budapest, where I began to take regular lessons. I changed teachers often. I went from the Hungarian school to the German school, and then to the Franco-

Belgian school. I studied Ševčik's hundred thousand manners of bowing, and understood very quickly that technique was fundamentally an opinion, that each teacher tried to denigrate the efforts of his predecessor, and that in the case of a real talent such as mine, the confrontation between mediocrity and genius became even fiercer.

The years could be counted according to the size of my violin, which grew together with my hand. When I was twelve (and the instrument was at six-eighths of its regular size), I was in my fifth year at the conservatory, but, to be honest, there were by now not a lot of things the professors could still teach me about music, and so they emphasized technique. On the subject of technique entire volumes can be written, while on expression there is little or nothing to say. What, in fact, can be said about that ineffable state that springs from the union of physical force and ecstatic pain, when music, like a tongue of fire, expresses itself through man by searing his mind, its heat spreading throughout his body, possessing it, rendering it a pure means, dead to itself, entangled like a jewel in the billowing clothes of a god? Who could penetrate and reveal this secret? Among those I knew, who was capable of even suspecting its existence? So the professors took refuge in technique, because of its visibility and its tangibility, because it is made of nerves and muscles, because it can be endlessly debated and discussed. But only later, when I attended the Collegium Musicum—considered at the time to be the most important music school in Europe—did I discover that technique could also be used to torture and humiliate.

MUSIC, THEN, was my religion. But even the most steadfast faith can be shaken by doubt. One of my recurring fears, besides the destruction of my violin, was that I could gravely injure myself in such a way that I could never again use my hands. For this reason I didn't dare participate in games at school and was considered a snob by my classmates. But no matter how careful and protective I was of my hands, there was nothing I could do to reassure myself that I wouldn't fall prey to some mental disease. Everything I had learned was in my head. And added to these earthly fears were metaphysical and theological doubts. When I was dead and had entered the world beyond, would I still be able to play? If everything, after death, was reduced to pure spirit, what material would my violin be made of? And in a place of perfection such as Paradise, wouldn't flawless playing be commonplace? Would Hell be the only place my music would still be appreciated? In order not to leave my violin behind, would I have to compromise my soul?

But the most absurd doubt that would seize me late at night, provoking hours and hours of insomnia, was caused by the observation that music existed only in the moment in which I produced it, and that it deserted me every time I lifted my bow from the strings, without giving me any reassurance that it would return. I would have to get out of bed and go pluck the violin strings just to make sure that they still vibrated, that the music was still there, present, even if a bit sleepy, and would fully awaken when I so desired. But then I would ask myself: once the music came back, would it still be the same? How often it happened that my state of being, my mood, would weigh so heavily on me that the music became unrecognizable. How often those strings, which only hours earlier seemed made of air or an even finer material, became deaf guts, crude twine. How many times my bow, instead of flying, became so burdensome it twisted my wrist as if I were holding a bar of lead, and my violin's voice became ungainly, shrill, and vulgar, a voice I didn't recognize. The conclusion these obsessive thoughts brought me to was that music required absolute fidelity, and betrayal would be punished by irrevocable abandonment and condemnation to hopeless solitude. But all anguish disappeared the moment I began to play. And so the only remedy was to extend my exercises for as long as possible, to play my repertoire, which was growing continuously, from first to last and then again from the beginning. In a very short time this routine brought me dangerously close to a physical collapse.

When they told me, I refused to believe it. I would not accept that music could in any way harm my health. In fact, I couldn't be convinced that my health was important enough to require the suspension of my musical studies and a separation from my instrument. But the doctor, having verified a weakness in my lungs, was categorical: absolute rest and fresh air. And, for the time being, no violin.

As a result, that summer my stepfather drove us in his new car, a Packard with shiny chrome and a blaring horn, to a hotel on Lake Balaton, where my mother and I were to spend the saddest of holidays. Once settled into the hotel facing the lake, I watched many people come and go, but I didn't make friends with anyone, much less the children my age. I was in a perpetual sulk. My mother read and embroidered, and I sat for hours and hours on the terrace in front of the lake, bored and doleful, while the others leapt and bounded around me. Their rowdy games did not succeed in bringing me out of my apparent apathy. I was very much engaged the entire time in going over my repertoire, note by note. I had a prodigious musical memory. I could both sing and play a piece of music after hearing it only once. I would repeat the notes silently in my head. Every so often, I inadvertently let slip a moanlike sound, which my mother mistook as a sign of impatience. But she was happy to see me relaxed, and was careful not to encourage me to participate in the other children's games. The doctor's orders had been strict: no strain of any kind, no excitement. His orders did not include the suspension of schoolwork, however, so in the afternoons, I was supposed to spend several hours on summer assignments. But I got tired almost immediately and passed most of that time lying on the bed thinking about music, my violin, and counting the days until I would be reunited with it.

THEN ONE AFTERNOON while I was in my room something extraordinary happened. Evening was already approaching, and I was seated at the desk with a book open before me, daydreaming, when all of a sudden I thought I was having an auditory hallucination. Was it possible, I asked myself, that by virtue of the intensity with which I thought about my violin's sound, I was able to make it materialize? I didn't know where it was coming from, but wafts of sound reached me, sometimes clearly, sometimes muffled, as if carried on gusts of wind. I leapt from my chair and ran to the window, but outside on the large terrace below were the same people as always. The sound then completely stopped, and after a moment I became convinced that what I had heard was only an illusion. But while leaving the balcony, I heard it again, at first just barely perceptible, then becoming as clear as ever. I thought that maybe the sound was coming from a gramophone in a nearby room, even if it was not that sort of music. Finally, by moving slowly around the room, I determined its source. There was no doubt that the sound rose and fell from my desk, just as if it were a music box being opened and closed. After checking in all the drawers and finding nothing, I realized that the music was coming from under the desk. I went down on all fours and figured out that the notes were filtering through a crack in the floorboards. I pressed my ear against the floor and now could hear the sound in all its clarity: it was not a gramophone but someone who was playing the violin in the room beneath mine. And it was the playing of a master. The notes flew without rest, without vacillation, with incredible speed: *staccato, portato, legato, puntato,* and then again in reverse, *puntato, legato, portato, staccato*. . . . He was doing Ševčik's exercises, that tiresome technique which in this musician's hands had become a virtuosity.

The sound's volume, however, varied. It rose and fell, and every time it returned, it seemed that the strings were vibrating a few centimeters from my cheek. I decided that the violinist must have been playing while walking back and forth. In an instant, the series of exercises stopped and up rose the beginning notes to Mozart's Concerto No. 2 in D Major: allegro moderato, andante, rondo, then again, andante. . . . I listened, immobile and ecstatic. Who knows what my mother would have thought if she had walked in at that moment! I stayed like that, stretched out on the floor, for I think more than an hour. Then the spell was broken.

That same evening at dinner, I looked around in an effort to discover the identity of the mysterious violinist, but the hotel, with its two hundred rooms, had nearly five hundred guests and three separate restaurants.

The next morning, gathering my courage, I went to ask at the reception desk for the name of the guest staying in the room that was right below ours. I was told in no uncertain terms that such information was restricted.

"I thought I heard the sound of a violin," I explained, in an attempt to appease the hotel employee, but he became even more suspicious.

"Did this occur during the night, perhaps?"

I was confused by his question. "No," I said. "It was yesterday afternoon."

My words seemed to placate him. "So you don't wish to lodge a complaint against Miss Hirschbaum?"

"Hirschbaum?" I asked, almost blinded by a sudden rush of blood to my face. "Sophie Hirschbaum?"

Thus I learned that the famous Austrian concert performer was staying at our hotel.

I DID NOT KNOW her, nor had I ever seen her before, but that morning, when she came to sit on the terrace only a few meters away from where I was sitting with my mother, I had no doubt as to who she was. I recognized her with that flash of foresight that causes us to remember a face even before seeing it, as if it had emerged from a memory that is not our own. She soon realized that I was staring at her and she smiled at me. She then seemed to avoid looking at me, but allowed herself to be observed, while consciously displaying a lazy indolence. Her pallor was heightened by a thick mass of golden brown curls, and her face itself, which was myopic and sweet and appeared at times to be in some sort of ecstatic immobility, had already filled me with deep emotion. In her virginal expression, I was particularly fascinated by her mouth, which suggested something rather painful, like a queen's suspicion that she is actually of plebeian birth. That must be she, I told myself. But I was only fully sure at the moment when she turned her head toward the waiter who had come up behind her, and I saw the brownish burn between her neck and jaw, that mark of a violinist who year after year leans a cheek against her instrument's hard ebony shell. There was no doubt that I was in the presence of Sophie Hirschbaum. And I had already fallen in love.

I couldn't wait another minute to meet her. Courage overcame me. I went without hesitation to her table, introduced myself, and told her that I, too, played the violin and was a great admirer of hers. I was a little embarrassed when she asked me on what occasion I had heard her play. I had to confess that it had only been the day before, when for a whole afternoon I had listened to her with my ear against the floor. She seemed amused, but also flattered, and suggested that I give up my uncomfortable listening position and instead come to her room for tea at four o'clock.

There, she said, I could listen to her play while pleasantly seated in an armchair.

Having obtained my mother's permission, punctually at four I knocked on Sophie's door. She herself opened the door and then led me to a chair, where I huddled in silence. Next to me was a steaming teapot, a bowl of sugar cubes, and a box of cookies, all of which I didn't dare touch for fear of making even the smallest noise. After I was seated, she did not seem to further notice my presence. She moved over to a table on top of which were two open cases with green velvet interiors, one containing a violin, the other a viola, and after a moment of hesitation, as if she couldn't decide which of the two to choose, she lifted the violin and began to play. The opening was limpid, crystalline, and I listened with my breath taken away by emotion. At first, I seemed to detect in her nervous movements a residue of childhood stubbornness, that same impulse that causes a child who wants something at all costs to stamp her feet and become red with rage until she gets it. But as the notes began to unfurl from her bow, she was transformed, assuming a severe, almost masculine expression. She remained like that in the center of the room, her back straight, her chin lifted in a gesture of disdain.

I felt that I would love her my entire life. It didn't matter that she was a grown woman and I was only a child, that there were more than ten years between us (at the time Sophie Hirschbaum was twenty-four years old and I wasn't yet thirteen). Nor was I worried by the fact that she would continue on her European tour, and I, instead, would soon be returning to Budapest. The roads where we would meet were not on any map, they were as ephemeral as the wakes of ships—ships that no matter how vast the ocean were still able to find the same routes.

At a certain point Sophie stopped playing and came over to me. She noticed that the tea had cooled and the mound of cookies remained untouched, but she did not say anything. She asked me whether I had brought my violin with me and if I practiced every day. I had to tell her about my unfortunate situation. "But soon," I added, "I will be going home and I can start studying again."

"It's a shame you didn't bring your violin," she said. "But there is something we can do." And she handed me her violin, the one she had just been playing, and she asked me to play her something. I looked at her hesitantly. Would I still know how to play after such a long time of enforced inactivity? I gathered my courage and lifted the violin, and although the instrument was a size bigger than mine, I gained back my confidence immediately. Almost as if in a dream, surrounded by the halo of her glance, I improvised for her some variations on a popular Hungarian melody. Sophie, with her viola, quickly placed herself at my side and supported my notes in counterpoint. And when the music dissolved on the dominant, we remained still, close, united by the same feeling. She looked at me in a strange way and then, squeezing my arm, kissed me on the mouth. "Don't ever give it up," she said. "Remember. You must never give it up!"

IT WOULD BE useless for me to try to make you understand how marvelous all this was for a boy like me. It was a magic moment. But that fantastic afternoon would not repeat itself. The next morning a group of excitable people arrived who, from what I understood, were Sophie's entourage and from whom, it was obvious, she had been trying to get some distance. But these people had little trouble locating and rejoining her. And now, having invaded the lobby with an exaggerated number of suitcases, monopolizing the elevators and bellboys, her small court—a garrulous, talkative woman, an old gentleman, and a middle-aged, pot-bellied man—was firmly installed in the hotel. Already they had taken it upon themselves to besiege her with advice, submerge her in recommendations and promises, and, while caressing her continuously, to flatter her to the point of exhaustion.

And then her suitor showed up. He had strong features, and his nervous but solemn gait was cadenced by an elegant walking stick. His unruly head of hair signaled the free spirit of an artist. Upon his appearance, the trio fled. Left alone, Sophie fought for a long while with him, at first in words, then in actions, her tiny fists vainly attempting to shake that insensitive chest, wrapped in a garish *gilet* made of cretonne and fixed by a bejeweled gold tiepin. In the semideserted lobby, he grabbed her wrist and tried to kiss her, but she managed to escape from him, taking refuge in an elevator, where, however, he joined her before the doors could close.

Only then did the trio reappear and gather around a table, where they remained in a melancholy silence as if they were at a wake. They were clearly worried about their pet, but none of them made a move to help her. I was beside myself with indignation. I wondered how in the world they could leave Sophie at that man's mercy, not lifting a finger to stop him. Desperate, I went up to my room, hurled myself on the ground, pressed my ear against the floor, and listened while he yelled the most terrible things at her.

Then, as hurriedly as he came, the man left. Having regained their courage, her entourage came up to Sophie's room and knocked lightly on her door. There was no response. The three knocked again and called out. Still, silence. The woman of the trio rushed to the stairs yelling, and after a while a maid came with a pass key. But the door had been bolted from the inside. Finally the manager himself came up, and after a few minutes two vigorous employees knocked the door off its hinges.

Immediately afterwards, accompanied by the hotel doctor, who had succeeded in stopping the bleeding, Sophie Hirschbaum was taken to the nearest hospital. Before slitting her wrists with a scissor blade, she had swallowed an entire vial of Veronal.

SOPHIE'S FOLLOWERS left along with her. I tried to get news of her all afternoon, but to no avail. In the next day's newspapers I could find nothing, and I had to wait until the following day to learn that she had survived. The article from the *Wiener Zeitung* attributed Sophie's gesture to a moment of crisis due to the interminable tour she had been on for over a year. That news put an end to my desperation and exorcised a mad bargain I had made with myself: I had sworn that as in life, I would follow her also in death.

A few days later we left the hotel, anticipating our return because the episode had also upset my mother. During the trip home I did not utter a word. I stayed for long periods of time with my eyes closed while swallowing my tears. Against the reddish background of my tightly closed eyelids, an extraordinarily clear image of Sophie appeared. And her lips still burned my skin. That trip might have been the most painful time of my life had I not been able to cling to the thought that soon I would be playing again. This already made me feel closer to her.

When I arrived home, I went directly to my room, only to discover that my violin was gone. Convinced that someone had stolen it, I ran in desperation to my mother with the news. But she did not seem at all disturbed by what had happened. She brought me close to her and in a solemn voice said, "You are now an adult."

For a moment I was afraid that she was trying to tell me that now that I had reached adulthood I would have to give up the violin, which until then had been nothing more than a game. I could already feel myself succumbing to despair when, following her glance, I saw posed on the table the violin that had belonged to my father.

"The time has come for this to be handed on to you," she said, hugging me. Just touching it sent a painful shiver down my spine. It was as if my body wanted to accommodate the violin by somehow adapting to it. My limbs stretched, my fingers elongated in order to wrap themselves around the fingerboard, and in placing my cheek in the hollow of the chin rest, exactly where my father had placed his, I suddenly clearly saw his image. As if struck by a bolt of lightning, I felt the enormity of the gift he had left me. In comparison with that perfect instrument, all my previous violins had been nothing more than toys. And when finally, after so much time, I began to play, I felt as if it were someone else making the strings vibrate, someone else who was at once inside me and who contained me. It was as if from that violin a mysterious spirit had sprung forth, an irascible genius, represented by that cruel, anguished face that I glimpsed across the surface of the soundboard, gasping as if he were about to be submerged in water.

I T W A S 1932, and I was thirteen years old. It was an important year. I had distinguished myself in my studies to such a degree that I was admitted into an international competition established in memory of the great Joseph Joachim. Out of two hundred participants who came from all over Europe, and after a series of progressive eliminations, in the category of young students without diplomas I won with full honors. The importance of this competition lay in the fact that the winner was given a scholarship to the Collegium Musicum, the dream of every young musician.

Not far from Vienna, the Collegium Musicum was, among the many roads that lead to Olympus, the most arduous but also the most direct. To receive a diploma from the Collegium meant having a place guaranteed in any large and established orchestra. Furthermore, the school had produced famous soloists, such as the very same Sophie Hirschbaum, and I, helped by chance, which at the time was still benevolent toward me, began to follow her trajectory. It was certainly not the difference in age, nor physical distance, that separated me from her, and I knew the only way to close the space between us was to gain recognition as a violinist. Only this would allow me, one day or another, to find her again.

Perhaps some day, I told myself, I would be able to stand beside her and play Bach's Concerto for Two Violins or Mozart's Sinfonia Concertante. Or, together with her, I would be part of a quartet on a perennial tour around the world. And already I could imagine the understanding looks we would exchange before every *attacco* and at every *da capo*. Already I could feel myself fly behind her, following the wave of her notes, coming beside her at times, to then let myself be carried off in her wake. Already I saw myself at the end of the concert holding her by the hand and bowing before an applauding audience.

At this point the man who said his name was Jenö Varga stopped speaking. Without our having noticed, the restaurant had emptied and the waitress was removing the outdoor tablecloths. She came over to let us know that they were closing but that we could stay sitting there for as long as we wished, even overnight. I had wanted to pay the bill, but Varga insisted, and before I could put my hand on my wallet he had already piled on the table a handful of coins that, after a rapid count, ended up in the waitress's capacious coin purse. We asked in vain for one last round. After the woman moved off, however, he hunched his shoulders and pulled from his pocket a small flat bottle of *Obstler* and, uncapping it, took a swig. Realizing his lack of manners, he begged my pardon, and having dried the top of the bottle with the palm of his hand, he passed it to me. I politely refused. He drank another few sips, but remained silent.

For several long and thoughtful minutes, he seemed to be listening to an internal voice.

Maybe, he said finally, if I had made some other choice, not only my life but also my death would have been different. I could have taken a much easier road, even if less dignified. After winning that very difficult competition, there were several offers for engagements in which I would be billed as an *enfant prodige*. My mother, however, did not want to give in to that sort of opportunism.

But who knows why I am telling you these things? It is ridiculous to talk about what could have been, when we know that life has only a single path—that which we have chosen. One thing, however, is certain: I was in a dreamlike state when I crossed the threshold of the Collegium Musicum. In fact, if I hadn't been blinded by my desire to emulate Sophie Hirschbaum and by my love for her, maybe my survival instincts would have warned me against entering that institute revered by the bourgeoisie in all of Europe. Of course, they had no idea of the life their children led or the mortal dangers they faced inside those walls—which were in fact the walls of a former prison. Its awful appearance, even if seen only from the outside and at a distance, should have been enough to raise suspicions of what went on inside that building. Talent's reward was not supposed to be a visit to Hell. Yet considering the terrifying aspect of that place and the equally horrendous personalities of its inhabitants, the only logical conclusion one could possibly arrive at was indeed the contradictory notion that all ability must be severely punished.

At the precise moment in which the large iron front door closed behind my back, I understood that the only way to make it out of that place would be by enduring to the bitter end every kind of humiliation, and by submitting to the will of whosoever wanted to stunt my growth. To go back was impossible. Such a renunciation would be considered an unpardonable defeat by anyone who, like me, had been privileged with a scholarship to the most renowned music school in Europe. I would have to successfully finish my studies there or die trying.

While I and two hundred other students waited single-file in the large courtyard for the roll call to begin, I felt, like a whisper I couldn't quite understand, a vague temptation. Only a few days would pass before

I better understood the true nature of that pull. What I had immediately perceived, and would persist in feeling for all the months and years I remained beneath that high-sounding vaulted roof and in that perennial atmosphere of haughtiness and dismay, was nothing other than the incitement to suicide.

TODAY THE ONLY trace left of the Collegium Musicum is a few weed-covered stones. I would need a detailed map in order to show you the exact location of that building, which was transformed into an ammunition dump during the war and was then blown to pieces before the arrival of the Allied forces. Fortunately, that horrible place has been obliterated, though not from my memory. Even at the time it was not easy to get there. It was situated in lower Austria, in the Danube valley, on the road from Stockerau to Tulln. It could only be seen from the train, because it was a long way from any main road. At a distance, it looked like a fortress constructed atop bare rock. From the inside, everything seemed turned in on itself and closed to the outside world. Only infrequent slits in the stone walls revealed a bleak and rocky landscape against a dark horizon, but these failed to give even the smallest sign of that human consortium we feared we had left behind forever. Within the building, the only open space—a gravel-covered courtyard—was reminiscent of a valley buried deep in the mountains and barely ever touched by the sun. The courtyard was encircled with porticoes under which stood bronze busts of illustrious former teachers reproduced in a size so large they looked like monstrous macrocephali.

We had access to this courtyard only twice a day, during the evening's recreational hour and at dawn for gymnastic exercises. The rest of the day we lived inside and were subjected to military discipline. Our rooms were depressing cells with only one small window, which was impossible to lean out of because it was too high and set in a wall that was thicker than an arm's length. The only place to sit in these cells was on the foldout camp bed, which, once lowered, filled the entire room, leaving one hardly enough space to stand. At nine o'clock in the evening, the doors to these burrows were closed from the outside, the lights turned off, and no one was allowed out until five the next morning, when we all gathered in the courtyard for calisthenics, summer and winter, no matter what the weather conditions. We were then rushed to the showers, which were housed in small wooden pens and were literal traps. In order to open the door one had to use a good deal of force to turn a serrated doorknob, which then set off a timed spring device that would lock any-one inside who took longer than the five minutes per-mitted to wash himself. Once the door snapped shut, the tardy one would remain imprisoned inside for the rest of the day, and when attendance was taken he was marked down for an unjustified absence. And woe to whoever dared to liberate him from the outside, because he would immediately suffer the same fate. Actually, no one ran this risk, because the Collegium Musicum was also a ferocious hotbed of competition, where everyone thought only of himself. Every mis-take had a precise value that appeared on the student's report card, and it took very little to risk expulsion. The rules and prohibitions were innumerable. You were not allowed to have in your possession any gold object, money, letters, newspapers, books that were not assigned by the school. It was forbidden to sing, talk, make noise of any kind. You could not lean against the wall or sit, even during the recreational hour. And the few times that we were allowed to sit, we had to remain erect without touching the backs of our chairs. We had to maintain this martial behavior at all times, and everything had to be done in a hurry, every change of location performed with the utmost speed.

At five-thirty, we all gathered in the refectory,

where, while standing in front of our seats at the tables, we had to recite interminable prayers and sing hymns and chants before we were allowed to eat our breakfast, which we were then required to finish within fifteen minutes. At six on the dot, we had to be in our cells. After making up our beds with scrupulous precision and hooking them back up against the wall—because, as I said, otherwise there would not be enough room to move—we practiced the violin for two hours in the poorest conditions one can imagine, with acoustics worse than if we had been in a tomb. Everyone did his exercises in the midst of the most disturbing dissonance. Sometimes the clamor sounded like thousands of birds beating their wings in an attempt to escape an approaching hurricane. At other times, there was a terrible roar as if coming from a burning menagerie. And all of this was accentuated by thuds from a stick inflicted on our doors by a guard who, with the precision of a mechanical puppet, passed up and down the corridor, first on one side, then on the other, assuring us of his vigilance. No one could delude himself, even for a moment, that he could relax. I do not believe anything I have known comes closer to the Bible's vision of Hell with its wailing and gnashing of teeth. At eight we left our cells and went to class.

The Collegium Musicum centered on music but included in its curriculum the same humanistic and scientific requirements as a state-run school.

The Collegium was separated into three distinct divisions. The section for the study of bowed instruments, where I was, was the largest, and was located on the southern side of the enormous building. On the same side, although isolated from us, was the section for students studying the pianoforte and wind instruments. Finally, on the north side was the boarding school for girls. We could discover no more about that place than one could about the life in a cloistered convent. Only in the evening, watching from afar, could we imagine that behind those lighted windows girls moved to and fro. And with great emotion I often thought that Sophie Hirschbaum had also been a long-term prisoner there in one of those cells.

FOR EIGHT MONTHS a year no one could leave the college except on Sundays, when, led Indian-file by a physical-education teacher, we were forced to go on long marches through the woods in order to exercise our lungs. Sometimes we saw a house or a small village, and while passing by, we looked on with envy at what appeared to be normal life. This was our only contact with the outside world, since our institute was fully self-sufficient and had its own laundry, butcher, and fully equipped carpentry shop. There was no shortage of plumbers, mechanics, stokers, cooks, gardeners, carpenters. . . . And, in fact, all of the personnel came from the little villages that we passed during our excursions. These men and women regarded us with both curiosity and indulgence, especially the women who worked in the kitchen and served us at lunch time. They lugged enormous pots around to the tables, filled our aluminum bowls with soup, and now and again looked upon us with compassion. Yet we were well dressed, well groomed, and apparently revered and respected by our teachers. Wasn't this the forge in which the future's concert performers, soloists, and orchestra conductors were being formed? Weren't we the privileged few who, from among the many who had knocked in vain on those doors, were allowed in? Nevertheless, it was clear that those peasants and workers would never have wanted to see their children inside those walls.

The teachers, on the other hand, were prisoners just as we were (it is often said that jailers and prisoners suffer in many ways the same fate). And in this case, it was actually so. You see, our music teachers, many of whom were old, had all once been students at the

Collegium. When they reached the end of their studies, something must have stopped them from taking flight. Perhaps the hard years of training had squashed their need to excel as well as their desire for freedom. They chose to remain safely between the massive walls of the Collegium, even if in the most unrewarding capacity. So they had their rooms (which were only slightly larger than our cells), their meals guaranteed, protection from the outside world, and they had unlimited power over hundreds of students. Could it have been this that kept them there? Power? And since they were minigods of mediocrity, their mission was to slow down, discourage, to make sure no one equaled, much less bettered, whatever skill they themselves had. They were compelled to lead you down the wrong path, to become a stumbling block in your way. And they had to inculcate you with one truth: that you could only ever come close to perfection, you could never reach it. It was not by chance that the Collegium Musicum's coat of arms, which was sewed onto the jackets of our green cloth uniforms, depicted Sisyphus pushing his boulder.

We saw the entire faculty only at lunch and dinner, since they ate at the same time we did and sat together on what we called "the stage"—a long table placed on a platform, a bit off to one side but from which they could keep us continuously under control. The glue holding this group together was the jealousy they felt for one another and the hatred they nursed for the students in general. As for individual students, their hate grew in direct proportion to the talent of each youth who fell into their hands. And they all, in agreement, did everything possible to make his life difficult, treating him first with indifference, then with arrogance, and finally with vexation.

MY FIRST TEACHER, nicknamed Professor Decrescendo, was a revolting man, fat and vulgar, with long curly hair that fell down his back like a wig. During our lesson he would keep time by banging his cane adorned with figurines against the floor, as if he were the court musician for the King of France. *"A tempo! A tempo!"* he would yell, beating his cane ever harder. Or in a falsetto voice, grotesque for a man his size, he would interrupt a student with brusque and arbitrary demands for intonation: *"Decrescendo! Crescendo!"* But since he didn't specify which note or which series of notes he was referring to, he succeeded in throwing even the most prepared student into a state of profound confusion. I became aware of his tactics the first time we met, when he asked me to play something, anything. I thought I would play a capriccio by Paganini that I knew well. After a few bars, however, he stopped me for no reason. He couldn't tolerate listening to me play the piece in its entirety. He couldn't tolerate the idea that excellence could exist in a novice who had come there to learn.

"Come here," he said to me in a tone that promised nothing good. I obeyed. "Let's have a look at this violin," and he took it into his fat hands, lifting it up to right in front of his nose, as if he wanted to smell it. "Mmmmh, mmmh . . . What does your father do? He's a meat packer? Mmmmh, mmmh . . ."

"He's not my real father, he's my stepfather," I quickly corrected him. "My father died in the war."

"And what did your real father do?"

"He was a musician," I lied.

"Mmmmh, mmmh, I see, I see," he repeated while examining the violin. "This violin seems too big for your hand, and when the instrument is too big for the player's hand, it is inevitable that the notes will fall off. You will have to practice, my little dove, you will have to practice a lot. Don't think that you already know everything. Speed to the detriment of intonation is the most common defect in those who believe themselves to be geniuses, as you do. For the next few months, and perhaps for the rest of the year, you will put this wonderful violin in its case, consign it to the appropriate place, and you will play on an instrument made in our own workshop by our own violin maker."

There was absolutely no truth in what he said. He was simply trying to provoke me. It was an odious action taken on the part of an odious individual who furthermore allowed himself to call me "little dove"! Never ever would I have given up my violin. I would rather die! Nevertheless, he won, and I had to put my precious instrument into storage, receiving in exchange a receipt as well as a glistening and anonymous violin. And from that day on Professor Decrescendo took care never to ask me again to improvise. Instead he nailed me with a series of exercises that had nothing musical about them, were even anathemas against musicality. Thereafter we faced each other with true animosity, and I was forced to play the most useless and torturous pieces, using an instrument that had the voice of a stuffy-nosed adolescent. He continued to be relentless, and our lessons became veritable fights. The first few times, when faced with his absurd and malicious observations, I was unable to control myself, but after a while I learned how to silently accept even the stupidest criticism, confident that as much as this person tried to distort reality, my talent remained unassailable. In fact, with time

I began to go along with him. "Maestro," I would say, and with this appellation his enormous nose would bead with sweat, "do you think these notes should be played with the point or the base of the bow?" Or: "Maestro, in your opinion, which finger position is the most suitable for this passage?" Naturally, I had to ask him simple questions which didn't require too much thought; otherwise, he would explode. I stuck to the obvious, asking his advice about things that were so apparent that anyone who was not blinded by his own vanity would have figured out what I was up to. But he didn't notice a thing. I think that in the end he actually felt a certain sympathy for me—so much so that after a few months he let me have my violin back.

You cannot imagine how difficult it was to adapt to the mentality and behavior of that place. And it wasn't enough to bend to the will of others; you also had to accept every kind of hypocrisy, engage in flattery, be willing to lie and to inform on your friends. It was the only way to survive.

With each year things got worse. Every step we climbed, the ladder only became steeper and longer. A new teacher was no better than the one before; he simply used a different strategy, playing on different emotions. He didn't blast you directly like the last, but he circled around you, became your friend, praised you, encouraged you to reveal yourself, to confess, to tell him everything you felt about his predecessor and his teaching method, only to then blackmail you and, worst of all, threaten you with expulsion from the school. And the more progress you made, the greater the danger became. After a while, I felt relatively safe; I learned how to play their game. But how many of the others proved themselves to be so much less shrewd than I! At the Collegium Musicum the only type of punishment was corporal, and that was reserved for the youngest students. They were pulled by the ear, to everyone's general amusement, or they were locked in a bathroom for entire days; but at least they had the consolation that once they had served their time their debt was paid in full. For the older students, things worked differently: after one demerit a huge threat hung over their heads for the rest of the year. Only at the end of the summer session would the guilty party learn his fate. And the sentence would be pronounced in public, when all of us were present in the great auditorium during the graduation ceremony. After the various speeches given by the teachers and the interminable one given by the director, came the distribution of prizes and punishments, beginning with the punishments, which were always expulsions. The student's name was called out and he was invited up to the lectern. Once he heard the sentence, he had to remove the green jacket of his uniform, let it fall to the ground, and then leave the room as everyone watched. A death sentence followed by a walk to the gallows could not have seemed much more horrible.

But when I looked in the eyes of all of the students who witnessed this humiliating spectacle, all I could see was pitilessness. It was a coldness that I had felt myself sometimes when I heard news of someone's misfortune. It did not come from a lack of sensitivity or indifference but was simply a defense against death itself. It could have been my turn, but it was someone else's: this is what I saw in their eyes. This is the sensation I myself had. And our coldness only increased if our unfortunate classmate did not accept his condemnation with dignity—when he tried in some way to defend himself with tears and protestations, by planting his feet on the floor, refusing to leave, or when dragged out of the auditorium by force he still dared to beg for mercy. The coldness became ice when the guilty party threatened suicide, or, worse, if this threat was carried out, which happened three times during my tenure at the Collegium. We learned of two of the students' deaths only many months after they had left, but there was one who came to his decision on the spot. He made a superbly dignified exit from the auditorium, earning our admiration, walked unseen straight to one of the building's balconies and, with the same pride, hurled himself off. There was, however, the disturbing case of a student who exactly one year later, having earned the highest grades and honors, and with a future entirely guaranteed, came to the same end. We couldn't understand how both failure and success could lead to suicide. None of us remotely suspected how slight the divide was between us and death.

PERHAPS YOU are asking yourself how with this regime of terror the Collegium Musicum could enjoy such fame in all of Europe. How was it possible that a school in which all emerging talent was crushed still succeeded in producing accomplished musicians? At first I believed that this approach was part of some preconceived plan. I thought that by questioning your every certainty and constantly instilling you with doubt about the adequacy of your training, they actually wanted to build you up, free you from self-satisfaction, from presumptuousness, from vanity, in order to make you into a true virtuoso, a musician who would be smiled on by fortune, in accordance with the college's motto: *Virtuti Fortuna Comes.* But this was not the case. We were simply in the hands of ignoble men.

And yet the great teachers of the Collegium Musicum were constantly praised. "Great students trained by great teachers" was often said about the school. But there was no way that these great teachers were the ones I saw every day, those wretched souls who could never pass up an opportunity to nitpick among themselves over the most futile things, liars who didn't dare to pick up a violin themselves and yet spoke to you of notes and positions, who could eternally lecture you on the exact angulation of the first phalanx of your pinkie, but who would never speak to you of music, and who never would have played music in front of you so as not to expose their paltriness. They were not teachers, but various personifications of doubt, fear, and deception. They were vices that attacked your virtue. They were the infernal guards who blocked you from finding a way out of the circle of Hell you happened to be in.

Nevertheless, though we found ourselves in the kingdom of the lower deities, it is also true that Orpheus himself had once made this descent, and had placated the underworld gods and their guards by arresting all torment with his music. Even Sisyphus' boulder remained suspended on its slope. And during his visit Orpheus assumed the face and features of Enescu, Flesch, and Hubay, the era's greatest violinists—the equivalent of today's Menuhin, Oistrakh, and Ughi—who were guests at the Collegium Musicum in the late spring. They gave their seminars and ended the scholastic year with great enthusiasm, causing us to forget every injury and humiliation, because during that four-week period music was finally present, and the very grayness of the building and each of its inauspicious influences disappeared completely during the time of their stay. It was this alone that induced us to return the following year.

IN THE SUMMER, school finished and we went home. My encounter with the outside world almost irritated me. I lived my vacation as if it were some useless waste of time. During those eight months of imprisonment my mind had become accustomed to severity, to discipline, to the pursuit of perfection. I suddenly felt as if I were a stranger among all those noisy people who had nothing to do with music, talked about everything but, and were concerned with things I didn't understand. At home my time was exclusively dedicated to practicing my instrument. Everything else was foreign to me, and I too appeared foreign to others. Even my mother said she didn't recognize me anymore. On my last visit, she too seemed changed to me. She had gained weight and there was something odd about her. She hardly ever got out of bed, and sometimes she implored me to stop playing, as if the sound of my violin was torturing her. I was mortified. That sound was my life. If I hadn't been so absorbed by my ambition, perhaps I would have realized that she was pregnant.

It was upon my return to the Collegium, at the beginning of the first trimester of my fourth year, that I received a telegram from home. My stepfather begged me to come home immediately because my mother was not well. I traveled all night and arrived at dawn, though the lights on the first floor were still on. As I climbed the stairs, I bumped into a woman carrying a basket full of sheets drenched in blood. I found my mother lying in bed with her head supported by two pillows. She didn't recognize me. She had been unconscious for two days. Every once in a while she opened her eyes, but she had no idea who was in the room or even how many of us were gathered around her bed. That morning a priest came to administer extreme unction. And after a few hours someone, using the palm of his hand, pressed her eyelids closed.

Everything happened in front of me, and yet it was as if I were somewhere else. I felt no pain. It was as if I had become encased in glass. My soul had left me and only my rational self observed with a detached eye every detail. But reason doesn't recognize sorrow. If I felt anything at all, it was an uneasiness due to the fact that I would have to set aside my violin. At a time when I should have been thinking only of my loss, I lived the event as if it were an annoying accident that took me away from my practice. For the entire duration of the funeral rites I would not be able to dedicate myself to my music. Even with my mother laid out in her bedroom to be mourned over, I couldn't resist the temptation to touch the strings of my violin with my bow to hear at least their whisper.

This alone will allow you to understand how twisted my mind had become by then.

MY MOTHER was buried, as she had wished, next to her parents in Nagyret. It rained during the funeral. The two coffins were lowered into the grave: first my mother's dark one and then, on top of it, a tiny one varnished white for the creature who died during birth and in dying took my mother's life. It all happened before my eyes with an incredible rapidity and precision. Every move, although obviously necessary, seemed to me to be carried out in a brutal fashion. The sacred act of interment took place in a great hurry. I was expecting that the earth would be sifted into the grave a layer at a time between elegies and prayers, that it would be placed delicately over the coffins, as with the sowing of seeds. I found it intolerable that, instead, stones and clods of dirt were thrown in with such force that they resounded like the blows of a rifle butt against a door in the dead of night.

AFTER WE returned to Budapest, my stepfather called me into his office. With him was a small man dressed in black, a notary who was to witness the reading of my mother's will. She left me a sum of money and asked that my stepfather give me an annuity until I came of age. When the notary had left, my stepfather assured me that he would respect his wife's wishes. He said exactly that: "my wife," not "your mother," which he had always done previously. He added that for the next five years, until I turned twenty-one, he would pay for my studies and support me by giving me a yearly allowance sufficient to my needs. He then gave me an address in Vienna where I could go to collect the sum. He said he knew there was nothing now to draw me back to his house, but he announced that he would always be willing to welcome me into his business, if I ever so desired.

"I know that you never considered me a father," he said, "but I loved you. And though I also wanted a son of my own blood, you cannot blame me for her death." He then began to cry. The tears that dried on those round cheeks, smooth as river stones, caused me to feel blindly jealous. As hard as I tried, it was impossible for me to imagine that this man could have loved my mother. And while he was at the height of his emotion, bent over his desk hiding his face in his arms, I stared at the wall above him, on which hung the advertisement sketch for a new product: pork pâté. Gathered around an open can, an entire family, each with a rosy complexion and obese, from the grandfather to the infant sitting in his high chair, exhibited the most abject happiness.

THAT SAME afternoon I left for Austria. I returned to my place of atonement, and it seems that for days I didn't remember a thing. All that passed through my head were sumptuous images of the funeral, but they were devoid of all emotion. I saw over and over again the oak coffin cover close over my mother's profile, and I heard the continuous echo of the stones hitting the soundboard of her coffin. Then one day the hard glass surrounding me cracked, and everything all of a sudden took on its true significance. My violin case would shut or I would hear the rain falling and imagine it soaking into the earth. I would smell the perfume from certain flowers and that day would come back to me, at first only in bits and pieces, then more and more often, and I would feel intolerable pain for long periods of time.

It was in this mood that I took up my studies again. That year, as never before, I was tempted many times to abandon everything and go work for my stepfather's company. It was the most difficult year, the year in which the doubt that music was not a good enough reason to live made itself felt ever more intensely. It was the year in which music itself, which up until then had consoled me with its immaterial presence, completely abandoned me. I discovered the cold structure of technique—*corpus sine spiritu*—automatic movements that brought about diatonic scales, chromatic scales, dissonances, melodies. And yet beyond all of this there was an obstinate silence.

Once Again my storyteller interrupted himself. I don't know why. Perhaps it was the noise made by the mechanical street sweeper moving down the street, dazzling us with its spinning light. Or maybe it was a car door slamming and the voices of friends saying good-bye. Whatever it was, his train of thought was broken, and he seemed to be searching for where he left off by anxiously rifling through his pockets. Finally, he pulled out the small bottle of schnapps, drained the last sip into his mouth, and looked at me strangely. There is often a moment deep in the middle of a performance when an actor returns to himself, or when the narrator of a story suddenly quiets and looks you in the eye. He was staring at me now as if he had just woken up from a dream. Maybe he was trying to remember who he was and what he was doing there, sitting across from me, at that hour of the night. I was afraid he might want to leave, but I didn't say anything, because at that moment any movement, any word, would have been out of place. For a while he seemed to be examining my expression in order to find any trace of incredulity. I must have passed the test, because all of a sudden he laughed. It was the first time I saw a smile—even if bitter—on his face, in place of the usual insolent sneer.

Almost in a whisper, Varga resumed his story:

During that year I made my first friend, whose name was Kuno. I came to this, I believe, in order to get through the last and most difficult stretch. As you will have already surmised, in that climate of disloyalty and betrayal it was rare, if not impossible, for friendships to form. In addition, every relationship was poisoned by suspicions of homosexuality, and the natural sympathies that grew between students were systematically discouraged by the teachers. Any sympathies that did develop, however, cooled when the time came to put together a chamber orchestra for the last concert of the year, in which a famous soloist was invited to play. That concert was our only possibility of meeting a celebrated musician face to face, and we would make ourselves known to him at every opportunity, so that one day we might be able to use his acquaintance to our advantage. In fact, at the Collegium, it was just about everyone's ambition, once he had finished his studies, to become the personal student of a great musician. And the great violinists were notoriously disposed to teach only those who had shown themselves already to be maestros. Therefore, the final concert became, even if indirectly, a veritable audition. The ensemble for the chamber orchestra called for only fourteen violins. Places were limited, and everybody competed for them. Halfway through the year, the tension was already so great that many students avoided talking to one another altogether.

It must be said that in an atmosphere such as that one, all attraction was determined by artistic affinity. The reasons why two students were drawn toward each other were purely musical in nature. The language was music. The subject of every conversation was music. Everything was music at the Collegium. But music could profoundly unite as much as it could profoundly divide. The intensity of my initial meeting with Kuno—which came about in a very singular manner—didn't allow for division.

In general, the faces, voices, and names of the

classmates one was chaotically surrounded by quickly faded into forgetfulness. They all became confused, to the point that you could suddenly become aware of someone's existence even though you had spent months and months seeing him every single day. But only when you heard him play did that "stranger" assume a precise physiognomy.

Which is exactly what happened between me and Kuno. He made himself known to me for the first time one day during morning practice. In those two hours, we were allowed to choose what we wanted to play. Each of us tried in that cacophony to concentrate on his own notes without being overwhelmed by those of his companions. That particular day I was tired and exasperated by the silence that had been reigning inside me for some time. I had been forcibly hurling myself at music, like someone who after knocking in vain on a door decides out of desperation to ram it down with his shoulder. I was fervidly playing the capriccio by Paganini that I knew by heart. The energy with which I approached that piece was such that after a while I had the sensation that I was all alone. I no longer heard anything around me, every clink and clang had suddenly stopped, and I was the only one playing. It even seemed to me that my own notes were rebounding from a distant echo. After a little while,

I realized I wasn't hallucinating, that all the others had actually stopped playing in order to listen to me, or to be more precise, in order to listen to us. Yes, because someone in a cell contiguous with mine was playing the same piece in unison with me. And when I quit, a bit taken aback by how quiet it was around me, the echo did not immediately stop, but continued for a few more beats. Then the silence was nearly complete. This someone was waiting to hear if his signal had been received. My response was to start playing again, picking up at the place I had left off. And right away this other person's notes repeated mine, mimicking me. But the entire episode was brief. The guard was already ranting and raving up and down the corridor, furiously beating his stick against the cell doors, commanding that we continue to practice. And after a few seconds, the clamor of the bows submerged us once again.

This was only our first encounter and not enough to make us recognize each other. We were simply voices seeking each other out. But a few days later, while I was walking down a corridor on the way to my usual afternoon lesson, I heard behind a door someone who was vehemently playing the violin to the maximum beat of a Maelzel metronome. I opened that door without any hesitation, without thinking of the disastrous consequences my interruption might produce. Fortunately, the boy was alone. He didn't notice me and continued to play.

For an instant I froze. The boy looked like me: he was my age, had the same body type, the same hands, and above all the same rapt expression I felt was imprinted on my face when I played. I thought I was looking at myself, as if that room were covered in mirrors reflecting my image back to me. And I saw in him my double, a replica of my emotional self, the part of me that is the unappreciated understudy who from time to time asserts his claim on the pale mask that struts about on stage. And I saw myself, my life, crucified to my violin. In that moment I understood all the obsessive and possessive power of music.

But the mirage vanished almost immediately. The boy, now aware of my presence, stopped playing and turned toward me. He didn't seem at all surprised. In fact, he smiled and came over to me, holding out his hand. Then I saw that he didn't look a thing like me. "Kuno," he said. "Kuno Blau. It was you that day . . . who sparkled."

"And you no less."

He pushed me firmly out into the hall. "Go now, before my teacher catches you here." Before closing the door, he paused briefly and smiled. "It sounded like the song of sirens in the middle of a storm." He winked and pulled the door shut, giving me barely enough time to get away without being seen by the teacher, who was approaching just at that moment.

KUNO WAS BORN in Hofstain, in the Tyrol, and had studied at the Innsbruck Conservatory. But his parents wanted him to get his degree from the Collegium Musicum, requiring Kuno to pass a difficult entrance exam and to enroll for the final two years. His parents were aristocratic and well off—his father was a banker—but he didn't enjoy any privileges over the other students and, in fact, behaved just as if he had been there from the first term. He did stand out, however, due to his unwavering display of confidence accompanied by a hint of arrogance, even in front of the teachers. What I liked about him was also the fact that, reinforced by this superior attitude, he often rose to the defense of the weakest, something never seen at the Collegium.

I remember one day we were watching a rehearsal—the upper-level students were allowed to observe the lessons of the younger students—for a concerto grosso by Handel. In the ensemble was a boy who was often picked on by the others because he was emaciated and had fire-red ears that sharply contrasted with his pale complexion. When they began rehearsing again after a brief interruption, the boy's violin started to make strange sounds. Who had done it or when, no one knew, but it was a common trick to render someone's violin unusable by rubbing soap on the strings. The boy futilely continued trying to play. His classmates were already giggling, or rather, gritting their teeth in an attempt to keep from laughing. But before the teacher could react, Kuno got up from his seat, went over to the unfortunate boy, who was about to burst out crying, and gave him his own precious violin, thereby allowing the kid to finish the rehearsal. It was an unexpected and disconcerting gesture. And from that day on no one dared to play a trick on the boy with the red ears.

Kuno and I were the best in our class and perhaps in all the school. What initially attracted us were reciprocal feelings of admiration. Although there was never much time for us to spend together, we often exchanged looks of understanding and complicity. We were by now among the elite. Although separately, we had overcome all the obstacles, passed all the tests. We could now look with confidence at the future and with a sense of superiority over all the others, who were still struggling in the lower depths. We were respected and admired. Even the teachers' envy and antagonism was transformed into a nauseating benevolence so awkward that sometimes it became intolerable. During our hour break we walked together in the courtyard while the others looked on. And naturally we didn't hide anything from each another. I told him the story of my entire life down to the most minuscule details, even of my love for Sophie. But Kuno's world was very different from mine. If mine was empty, his was overflowing with things, people, memories. Instead, in my background there was nothing, not even a father. And sometimes this made me feel jealousy toward him, but mostly I simply admired him.

For the year-end concert we were the two violins chosen to play in Mozart's "Dissonance" Quartet with the great Piatigorsky on the cello. And a few days later, while saying our good-byes until the fall, there was already the promise of a continued friendship.

THAT YEAR for the first time I left the Collegium without having any place to go. This freedom was dizzying. Just the thought of having to return in a few months inside those prison walls made me sick. At the same time, however, I considered that place my only refuge. The outside world was made even more vast by loneliness and more empty by freedom. The offices and warehouse of the new branch of my stepfather's company were located on the mezzanine floor of a brick building on the Wienzeile in Vienna. His pâté dominated the Austrian and German markets, and the obese family from the advertisement was smiling happily on all the walls of the city with the slogan *"Schmeckt Gut?"*

My stepfather had instructed the branch manager, a Mr. Peter Grenze, to give me a sum of money for living expenses and asked him to help me in the case of any other need. Mr. Grenze gave me the addresses of inexpensive rooming houses and student hostels. Then, perceiving my reluctance, he suggested the comfortable attic of a property he owned on the Schülerstrasse, where I could play the violin even at night without disturbing anyone, and I would also be, he added, only a few steps away from the house where Mozart had lived. Naturally I accepted his offer, and thus found myself a safe haven. My dormer window looked over a courtyard where a stonecutter worked. Slabs of marble were strewn about along with angels carved out of stone. And sometimes in the evening I heard notes from a piano and the impassioned voice of a baritone coming from the window below mine.

For four hours a day I practiced the violin; then I

took a long walk until I reached the banks of the Danube, where I lay down on the grass in the sun and watched the barges go up and down the river. I ate pastries or stopped at a food stall. I lived the life of a Bohemian and sometimes, even in my solitude, was happy.

I had not forgotten Sophie Hirschbaum. In the four years that I had spent at the Collegium Musicum, I had followed her from afar through newspapers that were passed about clandestinely. Sophie Hirschbaum was Viennese, and the Austrian press wrote about her often. By placing the dates of the news about her in order, I was able to make myself a map, albeit incomplete, of her movements around Europe. After the dramatic episode on Lake Balaton, Sophie had resumed her concert performances with a renewed dedication, although in the past couple of years she had slowed down a bit. Perhaps, having liberated herself from a demanding contract, she now alternated her concert activities with studying and teaching.

You can imagine my reaction, then, when I read in the paper that the following year she would be holding a series of seminars in Vienna for a small group of young graduates. I had exactly one year left until the end of my studies. In the meantime, I would write to her and tell her of my wish to meet with her. I was overwhelmed by the idea that destiny had so perfectly converged our two paths, just as I had always predicted. The newspaper, however, gave neither the place nor the dates of these seminars. At the conservatory no one could tell me anything either, and when I insisted on knowing where I could send her a letter, they gave me the only address they said they had: 19 Bürgerstrasse in Vienna. On that rather quiet and secluded street I began my patrol. I would walk up and down it for hours, holding my violin case. I got the distinct impression that the few people I ran into suspected my motives for roaming the area. If the first day I remained on the far side of the street and only allowed myself a glance from a distance at the house with the number 19 on it, by the third day I went right up to the front door in order to read the names of the inhabitants written above the doorbells. Sophie Hirschbaum was not among them. I looked again and again, but her name was not there.

"Who are you looking for?"

The man who had made me jump by coming up behind me without my noticing had white hair and a pale complexion. He evidently lived in that building and was about to put his key in the lock. He decided not to, however, and continued to assess me, observing with particular interest the violin case I was carrying.

I had nothing to fear. After all, I was only doing the most legitimate thing in the world: looking for someone. And yet those in love, like thieves, always have something to hide. So, in response to his question, I pulled from my pocket a piece of paper on which the address was written and, waving it in front of him as if it were proof of my good intentions, I began to stutter something about a seminar in musical studies that was supposed to take place in Vienna under the instruction of Sophie Hirschbaum. The old man had finally decided to insert his key in the lock and, opening the door, he motioned me inside. At first I hesitated, then followed him through an entrance hall and up some stairs until we stopped on the first floor in front of an apartment door with an oval nameplate made of brass badly in need of polish on which was written "Prof. Albert Ganz." The man was panting from the flight of stairs, and a little color had returned to his ashen cheeks. He had not said a word since we entered the building, and I wondered why I had followed him as far as I had. Still silent, he was struggling with a bunch of keys in an effort to open this lock, an operation that appeared more difficult than the first. I decided right then to ask him if he was involved in some way with Sophie Hirschbaum and her course. He looked at me with a smile at once good-natured and sly and made a barely perceptible nod in the affirmative. In the meantime, the door opened onto a dark and bare hallway with a gaudy gold metal umbrella stand and a few vases filled with aspidistras. Again, he motioned me inside. I followed the old man to the end of the corridor, where an open door appeared to contain the apartment's only source of light. Once through the door I found myself, to my relief, in a large and luminous dining room. At our appearance, a canary in a cage began to twitter insistently, and the man, as if he had been reprimanded, spoke to it in a singsong voice while he changed the water in the birdbath and added fresh millet to the tiny food dish, continuing all the while to apologize ever more profusely to the little animal for having been out for so long. It was not difficult to understand that the man lived alone and perhaps had been doing so for too many years.

All this time I remained standing at the doorway, observing with amusement his attentions to the bird, but when he disappeared through another door, I felt a little uneasy. For a moment, I considered the possibility that he had completely forgotten about me. But after a few minutes he returned, carrying two huge leatherbound albums, which he placed on a table. He looked at me for a moment, startled to find me still standing at the door. "Come in, my boy, and sit down." I avoided the couch and chose a chair with a rigid back. I continued to wonder what I was doing there. Then I saw something that heartened me: in an adjoining room no smaller than the one I was in sat a baby grand piano. I was in the house of a musician, or at least in a place where music was played. Of course in Viennese houses pianos were not lacking, but most, over time, lost their true purpose and were degraded to the role of a precious but useless piece of furniture. This one, however, had a score on its music desk, and its lid was raised—a sign that it had been played recently. The man was searching for something, opening armoires and chests of drawers, snorting and puffing loudly and swearing between his teeth. Finally, having found his glasses, he gathered up one of the two volumes he had brought from the other room and sat down on the couch right across from me.

He looked at me for a long time before he spoke. It was as if he were debating whether or not to confide in me.

"Do you know Sophie?" he asked me. I nodded, blushing a little.

"Once music was made in this house. But since my wife died and my only daughter has left to become a concert performer, I live only with the memories." And then, noticing my astonishment, he added, "Yes,

my daughter, Sophie, decided to take her mother's sur-
name, because she thought it better for her career."

He handed me one of the two books—an album of
photographs—and I began to leaf through it, at first
with curiosity, then with an emotional interest. Inside
was Sophie's entire life. I turned the pages very slowly,
looking at the pictures, reading the articles that her
father had collected and preserved. Four years had
gone by since the day we first met, but even in the most
recent pictures Sophie hadn't changed a bit. She still
had that delicate appearance of a pale and indolent
adolescent. I was struck by one photograph in particular, in which she was turned slightly away from the
camera, violin in hand, in a solemn pose suggestive of
an Egyptian divinity.

It was already late in the afternoon when Professor
Ganz asked me if I would like to play something
together with him. We went into the room with the
piano. The walls were covered with posters and flyers
from theaters all over Europe where Sophie had performed. After rummaging through pile upon pile,
stacked everywhere all over the room, even on the
floor, the professor found what he was looking for—
sonatas for violin and piano by Beethoven. We decided
to play the "Spring" Sonata, which he claimed to be
Sophie's favorite (and from that moment forth also

became mine). After he gave me the tempo, we immediately began the Allegro, and Professor Albert Ganz,
the absentminded and ineffectual man he had previously appeared to be, seemed to transform before me,
regaining all his youthful whim and inspiration. He
had a touch and a skill I would never have suspected. It
was as if we had been playing together forever. Every
pause, every *attacco* was precise, the chords perfect,
which I gleaned from his smile, from the winks he sent
my way, and from the rocking of his head, which at
times went so low it almost touched the keyboard. And
maybe, when he closed his eyes, he could feel Sophie
and his wife nearby. At the end of the Adagio molto
espressivo he got up coughing, said he was tired, but
that we would play again if I came back to visit. I put
my violin back in its case and let myself be led to the
door. Only then did I see that his eyes were wet with
tears.

I returned to that house several more times, and
before I departed for the Collegium, I left a letter for
Sophie with Professor Ganz, asking him in the eventu-
ality of a response to please send it to my stepfather's
company to the attention of the manager, Mr. Grenze.
But during the train ride I was tormented with doubt.
A letter is the most irrevocable thing there is, and
I went over and over in my mind each word I had

written. Hadn't I been presumptuous? My request to see her again in order to perfect my work under her guidance sounded as impassioned as a declaration of love. And then, had I made a mistake by reminding her of our meeting, which took place during a moment in her past that she certainly would have wanted to forget? But if, on the contrary, she had indeed forgotten that episode, then she wouldn't remember me, either, and my letter would read as if it were from some vainglorious fanatic.

I RETURNED to the Collegium with only a year left to go. But when a long journey is about to end and we are already in sight of the place we are headed, that last short stretch, so very brief in relation to how far we have come, suddenly becomes the most difficult of all. Distances seem to lengthen, and the destination gets farther and farther away until it disappears like a mirage. Kuno was a consolation to me. Our friendship during that year solidified, and we overcame every hostility directed our way. We were the top students, we were an example to the others, we were about to go out into the world as proof of the Collegium Musicum's greatness. Jealousy would not be disarmed; although others might ask which of the two of us was more talented, perhaps even trying to sow the seeds of discord, we ourselves never asked this question. Was it possible that the way to perfection could degenerate into a competition? Was it thinkable that the goddess of music could decide to reject one of us? We believed ourselves to be equal in talent. We progressed down the same narrow path, which kept us united, and we went forward guided by a single light. And if at the end of this path there was a door open to only one of us, then perhaps neither of us would enter, though each of us would do everything possible to push the other across the threshold, himself remaining outside. We were united in and by these feelings. How could we fathom a rivalry between us? We were like brothers, not in flesh or blood, but in that part of the spirit where order, rhythm, and harmony are found. I did not know yet that the spirit could darken itself.

The orchestra formation for the year-end concert called for only one of the graduating students to play the part of the first violin; and better yet, that part would definitely be given either to Kuno or to me. There would be no dispute, because I would gladly give up my place to him. I was not acting out of modesty, but out of supreme ambition. I made no effort to win the position in order to show my general excellence.

But when, halfway through the year, the news spread that the final concert would take place in Vienna and be transmitted on the Austrian National Radio, and that the soloist would be Sophie Hirschbaum, I had to think again about my feelings of altruism. The first violin in that concert could be played by no one else but me, the person closest to Sophie. Destiny would not want it any other way.

Life's temptations have the purpose of putting our spiritual integrity to the test. To yield to them, however, gives one a precarious and tormented satisfaction. But the worst temptations are those we give in to without getting anything in return except for the brutal discovery of our weakness. But, in fact, nothing of this kind happened. The whole program was suddenly canceled. Our conductor, who was also the concert organizer, was unexpectedly dismissed due to "health reasons," and within the walls of the Collegium strange figures who had little or nothing to do with teaching began wandering around. All of us, including the teachers, looked upon them with fear and suspicion. The new arrivals constituted a sort of "inspection commission" investigating the school. They were barricaded in a room on the first floor, but it was unclear exactly what they were doing. The only thing for certain was that interminable interrogations took place. Many of those who crossed the threshold into that room disappeared after a few days without a trace. Their names ceased to be called at morning attendance and were canceled from the registers. All that remained were their empty cells, their mattresses rolled up on top of the foldout beds. It all took place with such rapidity and decisiveness that in the end we wondered if Rosenbaum or Goldmayer or Horowitz—those with whom we had shared space, food, and knowledge for years—had actually ever been at the Collegium Musicum. But it was better to act as if nothing had happened, better to convince ourselves that they had never existed.

The "commission" were allowed to move anywhere they wished in the building. They could go into every cell, rifle through all personal belongings of the students and teachers, open the mail both on its way in and on its way out. Their power appeared unlimited. Someone said that the entire business had to do with the assemblage of a philharmonic of young Austrians and that the men of the "commission" had been instructed to put it together by choosing from various schools the best students, not only on the basis of their musical preparation but, it was rumored, also according to their political and religious beliefs. The year ended like all the others, or rather worse. The traditional seminars taught by famous violinists were not held, and the final concert was canceled altogether. Instead, we listened to lengthy speeches about music and patriotism, about the function of music in society, about the degeneration of contemporary music. Once again, the much-awaited meeting with Sophie Hirschbaum vanished.

IT SEEMED impossible that I could leave those walls knowing with certainty that I would never have to be enclosed within them again. But, as is often the case when one gets what one has desired after many years, I discovered that I had become so used to the restrictions and the struggle that I had almost lost sight of the goal I had so obstinately pursued. That which I had gained seemed already passed, already behind me. It was as if having fallen asleep on a train, I woke up thousands of miles away from the station at which I had intended to get off. Even before leaving the college, I regarded my classmates and teachers from a different perspective. I felt for them not only affection but also a bit of envy. I had to leave. They could stay.

Kuno wanted at all costs for me to come with him to Innsbruck as his guest during the holidays. But I had a few personal matters to take care of. Kuno persisted and made me swear that as soon as I had settled my affairs, I would come to visit him. I promised him I would do just that, and we departed in opposite directions.

Returning to Vienna, I went straight to my stepfather's company to pick up my small income. Mr. Grenze wasn't there. I was told to wait in his office, and I looked around with some dismay. The desk stained with ink, the bare walls, the chipped plaster and patches of mold along the baseboard, the frosted glass in the door, the window overlooking the warehouse . . . Was this the place I was destined for? While I was waiting, I read and reread the fire safety rules tacked to the wall next to the desk. I was especially struck by the part where it said to abandon the building in case of fire or any other danger "promptly but without panicking," and I tried to imagine how that would be done. I saw the rosy obese family pass by outside the window, its members smiling at me, as if they were inviting me to join them. The pâté advertisement was now being reproduced on the sides of the company's delivery trucks.

Finally, Mr. Grenze arrived. He seemed happy to see me again. He gave me what I came for, deducting from the sum the following year's rent for his attic. There was also some mail, he told me, and at those words my heart jumped in vain. The letter was not a response from Sophie but from my stepfather, who had somehow heard the results of my final year's studies and wanted to congratulate me and tell me that I should now pursue my adventures. I was young and talented and it was only right that I should go as far as possible toward realizing my ambitions. When he was young, he, too, had been a dreamer, but in the end the severity of life's difficulties brought him round to his rightful place. He concluded by saying once again that there would always be a position for me in his company.

From there I went to number 19 Bürgerstrasse in order to make sure that my note to Sophie had been forwarded, but a neighbor told me that Professor Ganz had gone and would probably not be returning. He had sold everything: his furniture, the piano, all the books.

"But where did he go?"

"He had the look of someone who was leaving for somewhere very far away."

"But why?"

The woman repeated "Why?" then shrugged her shoulders.

AT THE END of July I decided to accept Kuno's invitation and informed him by telegram of the day and time of my arrival. I asked Mr. Grenze to send any correspondence to Kuno's address, then departed for Innsbruck—unaware of the fact that I was being propelled on a journey into my past.

WHEN I ARRIVED, Kuno was waiting for me at the station with a car and chauffeur. The latter, a heavyset man in a gray duster coat with sunglasses resting above his forehead, took my suitcases and put them into the trunk. After a tortuous journey through the woods, the walls of Hofstain disentangled themselves from the black of the fir trees. Hofstain was not a village, as I had always believed, but a genuine castle. When we got there, the sun was already close to setting. The broad facade was in shadow, and the first-floor windows reflected the last ribbons of light from the sky. The car stopped in front of an enormous metal-studded wooden door. After unloading my bags, the driver, using considerable force, pulled a handle sticking out from the wall. A long, loud peal resounded inside the castle, and after an interminable wait the door opened and a valet appeared, wearing black velvet trousers that ended at the knee and pure-white cotton socks that wrapped softly around his spindly calves.

We entered. The interior was dark. In the distance a

single ray of sunlight pierced through faceted glass and galaxies of suspended dust, illuminating an astrolabe placed in the middle of a table piled with books and stacked with papers. The stale smell of time emanated from the austere furniture, from the tapestries, from the gallery of ancestors' portraits. Even Kuno's parents seemed to be already posing for posterity. His father was a tall man with a receding hairline and thick gray side whiskers. He corrected his lame stride with an elegant ebony cane. His mother was still a young and beautiful woman, with one of the most captivating smiles I have ever seen. She immediately made me feel more at ease by telling me that everyone at Hofstain was impatient to meet her son's friend. I was surprised by this "everyone." Who else was there in that castle? I would know soon enough. There was Kuno's aunt, his father's sister, a silent, thick-boned woman with gnarled wrists and hands, who always wore lace blouses closed at the neck with a cameo. And there was Kuno's paternal grandmother, the old Baroness, whom I came upon while she was being pushed in her wheelchair by a grim-looking governess. The old woman stopped a few feet from me and observed me by tilting her head slightly to one side in an odd, birdlike movement. A stroke had distorted her face, but I liked the extreme elegance of her attire and the whiteness of her carefully styled hair.

After introducing me, Kuno explained to his grandmother that I would be a guest at the castle until the end of the summer. He spoke in a loud voice and gesticulated as if he were in the presence of someone hard of hearing. In response to his words, the old woman made an effort to smile. "Gustav!" she exclaimed, but immediately afterwards, without any warning of the unexpected change except for a moment of excited astonishment, she dissolved into silent sobs.

Kuno took me by the arm and led me away. We climbed the stairs to the upper floors, and a little while later he showed me to my room. The shutters were closed, and only a dim light made its way through the slats. Kuno went to the window and, after lifting a hook, pushed wide open the shutter doors, which hit the exterior walls with a thud. A flock of birds rose from among the leaves of a poplar, and after a brief flight and a sharp change of course they returned to repopulate their branches. The grace and perfection of a bird's flight are a rare thing. I felt inside myself a sweet sense of calm.

Kuno appeared impatient to show me around. "You will have plenty of time to rest. Come with me now for a tour of the house. I wouldn't want you to get lost when you're alone."

He brought me to his room. Used also as a study and practice room, it was more furnished than mine, but it had also been left in a kind of picturesque disorder. I thought of the poor maid who had to dust in there without being allowed to move even the smallest object. There were bookcases crammed with books and scores, but there was also a rack of hunting rifles. Other shelves proudly displayed silver cups, medals, and plaques. Among these trophies, on the top of a bookcase, amid a set of rare books, there was even a skull, the color of ivory, with a lapis lazuli scarab set in an eye socket. It was a reference to eternity, Kuno told me, noting my interest. "It is the human spirit that crosses into the darkness of death," he said gravely. And seeing my gullible expression, he erupted into laughter and whispered to me that he had taken it from his uncle's office, explaining that his uncle had once been a doctor.

"Now let's continue before it gets dark." I followed him in silence, and as we passed through various rooms, he told me a brief story about each of them. It was the first time I had seen him outside the context of school, and already he seemed a different person.

"I can't show you all of them," he warned me, and

pointed to a door at the top of a set of stairs. "A few places up there haven't seen the light of day for at least a century."

The sun, by now setting, fractured through the half-closed window into myriad beams. The wood floors, laid out in huge squares, creaked with each of our footsteps, and blades of fine dust cut through the dimly lit rooms, flashing across the porcelain hidden in large glass cases, the faded boxes of pendulum clocks, the huge majolica stoves. And there was not a wall that didn't have hanging on it a deer's antlers, or a boar's head, or capercaillies and other stuffed birds, further revealing the Blau family passion for hunting. Kuno went ahead of me. With every door he opened, each step he took, I wondered how many times before he had done so in precisely the same manner. I am convinced that we leave invisible traces of ourselves on every piece of furniture, on every wall, in the house where we are born and grow up. For years light has projected our images onto those places where we habitually rest or which we pass by with great frequency. And something of ourselves must remain in those places. Kuno moved with pride through those rooms. He knew how far to push a key into a lock, the exact pressure needed to close a shutter or to lift a stuck door in its hinges. He was even familiar with each groan of the floorboards he walked upon.

After that rapid tour of the castle, he led me to the music room, where he showed me various instruments belonging to the family. There was a series of perfectly preserved violins, of which one was a Stainer and two were Albans, and a viola made by Klinger. There was also a Dutch harpsichord (the instrument his mother still played), a Guadagnini cello, and a number of ivory and boxwood flutes enclosed in a display case. Naturally, I did not recognize all of those names. I knew something of Stainer only because Kuno had mentioned him to me the first time he had seen my violin. He had examined it with great interest and had explained to me that it had been built by a violin maker who was born and had lived in Absam, a town not far from Innsbruck.

"My father also played the violin," he said, "before he was wounded by the explosion of a grenade."

He then opened a cabinet drawer and pulled out a violin bow. "Here," he said. "I want to give this to you as a gift."

At first I refused the present. It was, in fact, exquisitely made and obviously valuable. But he insisted that I keep it.

From there he led me back to my room, where he

described life at the castle and gave me some advice. To begin with, I was free to rise at any time I liked—he himself never came downstairs before midday—and if I were to get hungry, all I had to do was go to the kitchen or call the maid. If I got up early in the morning, I could go out for a walk or play the violin. At night, however, it would be better if I remained in my room, and I wasn't to be alarmed if I heard his grandmother scream. "For tonight," he said, "I'll have something brought to your room, but from tomorrow on you must never miss dinner, which is at seven sharp. It is the only occasion for which tardiness is not tolerated."

Finally, he left me alone. A little while later a maid knocked on my door, carrying a tray with bread, cold meat, and a bottle of water. I ate something of it and then, after emptying my suitcases, I pulled my violin from its case in order to try a few notes with my new bow. I stopped almost immediately, because the sound seemed to spread throughout the entire castle. I lay on my bed and stared at the high ceiling, which, in comparison with the minuscule amount of space in our cells at school, felt like the open sky. I wondered if I would be able to fall asleep in all that space. While I was lying there on my back looking around, I saw on the wall, above a bureau, the outline of a painting that had recently been removed. It was a ghostly absence, a space there had been no time to fill, and what remained of the painting was not only its well-defined profile but also the arrangement of a few ornamental objects, vases and fruit bowls, on the shelf underneath, which formed a futile embrace of the new emptiness. Perhaps it had only been a mirror, I thought, and while continuing to stare at that pale rectangle, I fell asleep with a sense of contentment, as if I had just returned home after a long voyage.

WHEN I AWOKE the following morning, I found that reassuring sense of belonging intact. In the turreted castle of Hofstain I felt at home. It was a feeling that mysteriously stayed with me for a few days. But soon, just as mysteriously, it disappeared.

I was so used to school discipline that I got up very early, and after having breakfast in the kitchen I found myself strolling about without any particular aim. Sometimes I reviewed the family portrait gallery or I sat in the library on a small couch purposefully placed directly opposite a large portrait of Kuno's mother, Margarete von Tumitz, whom the artist had ably reproduced in all her beauty.

The only other person awake at that hour was

the white-haired valet who, dragging his feet down the corridors and through the rooms, adjusted all of the pendulum clocks. Then someone would come out of the kitchen to feed the dogs. How many had run of the castle I never exactly knew. There was an old schnauzer that usually slept on the couch in the library, and two hounds that roamed deep into the woods during the day and often returned with some inexperienced hunter's catch clenched between their teeth (it was not rare to find pieces of bloody flesh on the floor and feathers flying everywhere). And finally, there was a pack of mutts, of all sizes and led by a bitch of frightful appearance, which went on rampages through the kitchens and living rooms, fighting and yelping, leaving the rugs and couches filthy, without anyone saying anything except for an occasional and tepid "The dogs should stay outside"—a precaution that was usually taken only late at night when the doors were locked. Some, however, were allowed to remain inside. The old schnauzer for certain, who after sleeping all day spent the night roving through the castle, and came sniffing and pawing at my bedroom door.

IN COMPARISON with the frenetic but disciplined life we led at the Collegium, time seemed to have stopped. Everything appeared to be enclosed in a crystal ball. The days passed incredibly slowly. Kuno practiced the violin in his room, and I in mine. We dedicated many hours a day to our instruments. From time to time when the weather was good, Kuno went hunting and was gone for the whole day. And during his absence I felt the increased awkwardness of a guest left on his own. Even if everyone, down to the last servant, treated me with courtesy and respect, I tried to keep to myself. If I came across someone, I greeted him and continued on my way, as if the corridors and rooms of the castle were the streets and squares of an unfamiliar city. The person who made me feel most uncomfortable was the Baron. And he too seemed to avoid me. He always had the demeanor of someone who was in the middle of dealing with something of great importance that he had been temporarily forced to interrupt, and when out of pure politeness he had to address me, the conversation was over after a laborious exchange of a few words. Each time he seemed to regret having engaged in a discussion that risked lasting too long. With an embarrassed smile he would glance at one of the pendulum clocks, put his hand over his watch without taking it out of his pocket, and appear sincerely disappointed that he didn't have time to talk further with me about such an interesting subject, one we would surely pick up where we left off the next time we met.

Kuno's mother, on the other hand, perhaps aware of my awkward feelings, hardly ever spoke to me at all, limiting herself to a simple "hello" accompanied by a reassuring smile. Often, unobserved, I found myself looking at her. When the weather was good, she sat out on the terrace reading or she went into the garden and paced back and forth on its paths as if she were waiting for someone. Sometimes, when she was sure no one was watching, her beautiful face became so saddened that I was overcome by a profound sorrow.

Kuno's aunt, together with the governess, looked after her infirm mother during the day. Only at night, after dinner, could she dedicate herself to her favorite pastime: playing cards.

BESIDES THE five members of the family and the servants, every day various visitors arrived. Some only stayed for dinner; others would spend a night or two at the castle. Dr. Egony, the family physician who administered to the old Baroness, came just about every day, and Monsignor Ciliani was practically a permanent guest. He was the Baron's usual adversary in chess. Their matches lasted entire afternoons and sometimes weren't concluded until after dinner. Often, during the long wait for the Baron to move his pawn, Ciliani's eyelids lowered and his head drooped forward. The Baron would tap him on the shoulder and the game would resume.

Around this group of people, who made up a fixed or recurring presence, circulated many other guests: relatives or friends, or friends of friends. Every Tuesday and Friday Mr. Klotz, the mayor of a nearby village, came to dinner. At the table there were always at least a dozen people. And Kuno's grandmother, always elegantly dressed and perfectly coiffed, never missed the evening meal. Food was by now her only pleasure. Paralyzed, she was fed by the governess, who took care of her both day and night. She could, however, with difficulty still move her left hand, sometimes to disastrous effect for the crystal and the precious tablecloth. And the governess would try to mop it all up with a napkin. On these occasions, the guests' discretion was admirable: no one seemed to notice anything, everyone looked the other way as if it had been commonly agreed upon to do so, and the conversation continued without even the smallest pause. The pretense went so far that someone, as if nothing had happened, would turn to Kuno's grandmother and ask her opinion on the subject of the conversation. Usually the old woman was not even aware that she was being addressed, and it was better this way. Sometimes, however, she would wake up and, staring straight in front of her, would pronounce the only word she was able to articulate with sufficient clarity: "Gustav, Gustav . . ." she would say suddenly, and mumble something incomprehensible.

At her outburst everyone seemed to freeze in his seat, and Kuno's mother appeared the most disturbed. "Gustav will come," she said to her gently, in an attempt to calm her down. But the old woman didn't pay attention. She continued to call out that name in a severe tone of voice, as if Gustav were actually present and she wanted to scold him for his unpardonable absence. Immediately afterwards she would lose herself again, and a tear would form in her right eye, the one that remained open even when she slept. Then, before she actually broke down sobbing, the governess with a kind firmness took her off to bed, and the old Baroness disappeared, light as a ghost. And other ghosts seemed to accompany her: gentlemen and ladies that had animated those rooms for centuries and whose voices perhaps she heard.

Even Kuno seemed to be listening to his past. I soon noticed that he was dominated by a real passion for his family history. He never missed a chance to talk to me about his ancestors, to show me their portraits, to tell me about their acts of bravery and their infamies. He felt obligated to explain to me every detail of the Blau genealogical tree, frescoed onto the library wall, where, among the others, I had already detected the name Gustav. I wondered if it was the same Gustav repeatedly cried out for by the Baroness. Kuno had never said anything about him to me, and I didn't dare ask.

Then one day my friend took me to the castle dungeons, where there were still cells with shackles and where a passageway, now walled up, led all the way to the banks of the river Inn. He told me stories about wars and revenge, about assassinations and betrayals. From underground we climbed a steep set of stairs built into the rock that ended in the open air next to the family chapel. The wooden door was barred shut, and on the wall above the architrave there was a niche containing an image of Saint Michael. Another gravely frowning marmoreal Saint Michael stood at the entrance to the cemetery, his sword pointing the way to the tombs. The area was encircled by a low wall and was on the edge of the forest. From that perpetually shaded place, the castle was set against the light, its edges brightened by the sun hidden behind its walls. The tombstones, standing at the head of rectangular mounds of earth and covered with fir-tree branches and wildflowers, were blackened by moss and, like the title pages of so many books, were adorned with the curlicues of wild vines. In the middle of the graves, and not at all frightened by our presence, two black crows haughtily stalked about. Kuno told me that he too, like all of his relatives, would one day be buried in that piece of ground.

My gaze landed on a fallen tombstone almost completely covered in weeds. No flowers or fir branches were anywhere near it. The earth in front of it, like a giant's footprint, was sunken. I went close enough to it to read the name Gustav Blau. I was not sure to what lengths Kuno would go to satisfy his desire to astound me with terrifying stories, but I understood that he had brought me to this place so that I would see that stone.

"Only Uncle Gustav," he said, looking in the same direction I was, "decided one day that this place was too small for him."

I shivered at his words. Since I was a child, I had heard stories about ghosts and the dead rising from the grave—legends about the walking dead did, after all, originate in Hungary—and this grave appeared to have been desecrated, or, although I hardly dared to think it, perhaps it had been forced open from the inside. I looked around with concern. The two crows took off, disappearing quickly into the thicket. Kuno was watching me as if trying to gauge from my expression the effects of his words. And while we were returning to the castle he told me the story of his uncle Gustav, his father's brother, who was a doctor and a scientist.

GUSTAV HAD DISAPPEARED mysteriously before Kuno was born. Some spoke of death threats, others of an impossible love. A few weeks later, a body was fished out of the river and, although unrecognizable, was identified as Gustav on the basis of a few particulars. His body, or the body presumed to be his, was buried in the family cemetery. But the dirt didn't even have time to settle before the casket was unearthed and the body stolen. The crime stunned everyone, and not long after, overcome with anguish, the Baroness was stricken with apoplexy and immobilized in a wheelchair.

"But I don't believe Uncle Gustav is dead," said Kuno.

"What makes you think that?"

"Still today among the servants the word is that my grandmother witnessed the body being exhumed. And more disconcerting still is that a few years ago a friend of the family, a renowned Austrian writer, who was visiting upon his return from South America, insisted that he had run into Gustav at a gas station on the outskirts of Bogotá, and that he had even spoken to him. Actually, it had not been a true and proper conversation: the man our family friend addressed had pretended not to know him, claiming that it was a case of mistaken identity, and quickly got into his Daimler (my uncle loved that type of car) and told the driver to leave. But our writer friend was ready to swear that he hadn't been mistaken. Some time later, the mystery of the death and resurrection of Baron Blau had inspired him to write a novel that had a good deal of success."

Death and resurrection? Kuno was exaggerating. It was a fact, he then added, that his uncle Gustav had always experimented with, besides medicine, alchemy. Mayor Klotz, who had been his friend when they were young, knew all about these practices of his. Hadn't he told the story, one evening when he had put back one too many, of participating in an experiment in which a teardrop of lead had been transformed right before his eyes into pure silver? And who had anonymously donated a considerable sum of money to the Blau Bank when, due to some risky investments, it was on the brink of ruin? Kuno's eyes shone as he spoke of these things.

"Uncle Gustav is still alive, I'm sure of it," he

concluded. "And he has accumulated an enormous fortune."

Perhaps one day the doorbell would ring more loudly than usual, the white-haired servant would open the door preparing one of his best "Welcomes," and Gustav Blau would appear just as everyone remembered him, or perhaps younger and better looking than ever, because, as is well known, the philosophers' stone not only has the power to transform metals but also can protect one from aging and perhaps even death.

Evidently, around the mysterious disappearance of Gustav Blau a legend had grown that was only enhanced by the years. The subject was never discussed openly at the castle, but was, in one way or another, often alluded to in conversation. At least this was my impression. Maybe the old Baroness was the only person who actually knew something. If she had been present at the exhumation, she certainly would have much to say about it. But for a long time now she had buried her secret in her aphasia. At times, it seemed she wanted to unearth it, but every impulse she had to do so was exhausted in that one word, in that one name. And in order not to invoke one of her crises, the conversations at the table concerned only the most banal and innocuous subjects. But as soon as she was gone, the conversation turned toward lofty matters, grand themes, the larger questions. It was not by chance that already from the first evening I found myself sitting at that table, the subject of life and death arose, and more precisely the search for immortality. This was a subject that usually pitted the positivist spirit of Dr. Egony against the spiritualistic nature of Monsignor Ciliani. Dr. Egony celebrated the triumphs of medicine. He predicted the defeat of all disease in the near future and the indefinite prolongation of human life. Often Mayor Klotz, a little man (his legs dangled from his chair like a child's) with red hair, a red beard, and a shrill voice, intervened, hot with anger. A goblin who decided to visit the world of humans incognito could not have found a worse disguise than his. Mr. Klotz objected to the positivism of the doctor, but neither did he share the prelate's spiritualism. Rather, he believed alchemy to be the only universal medicine and supported the theory of reincarnation. If both men were fascinated with hypotheses of how to achieve immortality, Monsignor Ciliani saw them as a terrible threat. And he even looked terrified. Transforming his regularly jovial appearance, his face darkened; his chin, compressed into his white collar, seemed to swell with all his disappointment; and his voice became thunderous, as if he were speaking from the pulpit. On that first night, in fact, I heard him cite a passage from Genesis: "Man has become like one of the gods, knowing what is good and what is evil. Therefore, he must not be allowed to put out his hand to take fruit from the tree of life also, and thus eat of it and live forever."

Humanity had been placed in check, the prelate maintained. In choosing the tree of knowledge, man had renounced the tree of life. And only death, or oblivion, could stifle his attempts at revolt. Once before, mankind had tried to conquer the heavens with the help of the rebellious angels, who would always contest their unsavory expulsion, and if God did not hold the power to immerse man in the sleep of death, he would remain defenseless before him.

THE BARON rarely participated in these discussions, but he had the power to put an end to them by rising from the table. His stiff leg rendered the maneuver somewhat difficult. He would fitfully push his chair out from under him, causing it to screech across the floor. At this signal all diatribes ceased and everyone repaired to the adjacent room for a game of cards.

Kuno and I, instead, betook ourselves to the music room, where we played duets for the violin fished out of innumerable unpublished scores that had been stored away, or, rather, stacked in a cupboard. Most of the music was worthless, written by dilettantes in order to entertain the nobility during the evenings. But Kuno loved it all anyway, and I went along with him. We rifled through dusty sheaves of paper, gnawed on by mice, sometimes illegible, and so worn out that a mere touch was enough to make them fall to pieces. We had fun interpreting that music with our bows, searching for something good for a small concert we thought of performing on one of the following evenings in honor of the guests.

Sometimes, however, we would stop playing and discuss what we had heard at the table. As I said, the subject of all subjects was immortality. Kuno had precise ideas, and his conclusions were definitive. His reasoning often seemed very strange, I didn't understand it, and it was pervaded by a cruel exaltation. Sometimes I was even frightened by it. According to him, through a hermetic axiom, everything that at one time had been divided would be rejoined. The past would make us great. Only the past could redeem us from paying the toll of death. The key to achieving immortality, that coveted human condition, was in the origins of our history. We were living a unique moment. Now, precisely in this age, the past was reawakening, like some thinking entity, and it was calling together an elect, and he who was chosen had only to let himself be led without fear. The choice between good and evil was obsolete and had been replaced by pure action, by pure progression down a predesignated path. The commandment was to return to our beginnings, to find the roots of the tree of life, to go back all the way to the first gods, to bring them out of the ice where they had been frozen, because our mortality was the direct consequence of their sleep, and once reawakened, they would see to it that we were made in their likeness.

Sometimes I felt Kuno was letting me know that he was in the possession of some secret, or that one day not long from now this secret would be revealed to him, perhaps even by Gustav Blau himself. He continued to tell me that nothing was lost of that which his ancestors had through great effort conquered. Everything was passed down through bloodlines or legitimate succession.

His words disturbed me. Wasn't ours an era in which godlessness and rebellion against natural and divine laws had extended all the way to the praiseworthy masses, to entire populations, which, enticed by the promises of a neighboring country, would give in to anything? For me this was a moment of darkness for the human spirit. I remembered the image above the door to the Blau family chapel: the archangel Michael stabbing a beast. Couldn't it be that humanity, in God's eyes, already resembled a ravenous hydra?

I let my imagination run freely. I discovered a world that I hadn't suspected existed. And for the first time I felt with anguish the emptiness of my life. For Kuno I felt an unusual jealousy, burning and painful, for his noble birth, for that castle in which history, in passing, had torn off a piece of its clothing, but above all for the support that he was given by a past that was continuously kept alive by the daily exercise of memory. In fact, everything in that place seemed devoted to this activity. It was a collective rite aimed at placing the deceased in an interregnum from which they could rise again. As a reward, they would spare those who recalled them the painful experience of death.

I FELT LOST. I began to think my friendship with Kuno had made sense only within the walls of the Collegium Musicum. There both of us had fought for years against a common enemy in the teachers; we were both constrained to kneel before the god Technique; we both struggled to deny the weight and rebellion of the bow. There we had been equals. But now something had changed. Kuno was different. He had begun to place a distance between us. Every time we played the violin together, he assumed the right to choose the part he liked more. He wanted to have his way all the time. When he was with me, he had a condescending air about him, especially in the presence of strangers. Sometimes he even forgot to introduce me. It seemed to me that he amused himself with this or that guest by pointing out my humble origins. Or he simply ignored me, as if I did not exist. Perhaps I had made a mistake by telling him of my grand ambitions. Maybe I should not have lied by telling him that the following year I would enter into a very exclusive circle by participating in Sophie Hirschbaum's music seminar. I had waited so long for a response from Sophie that finally I convinced myself I had actually received it, and I spoke of the whole thing as if it were already accomplished. But when we imagined our future together, it seemed as if Kuno reserved everything for himself, leaving only the crumbs for me. According to Kuno, the future would bring great changes. There would no longer be time for us to play the violin like cicadas. Other duties awaited us. Music, he said, could not be the only purpose in life. I knew he didn't actually think this way and that he was only trying to annoy and provoke me. For him, noble by birth, music would never become a profession. For me, perhaps yes. One day, while we were sitting at the dinner table, I heard him say: "Certainly music is life. And this is true for very many people. After all, playing the cello or the violin is an honest way to earn a living."

On another evening he made an even more poisonous comment: "We are living in difficult times. At best, our virtuosity can only lead us to exhibit ourselves in some spa." And then he turned to me. "What do you think, Jenö? At least there you could drink a few glasses of good water." I clenched my teeth into a smile, but I was tempted to get up from the table and leave.

Later, however, when we were alone, Kuno tried to fix things. He said he had only been kidding around, that he liked to tease me, and I almost felt remorse for having suspected him of ill will. I often asked myself if it wasn't jealousy that made me react the way I did. What bothered me the most was that I realized I could never really know Kuno. I found it unbearable that his essence escaped me, and I suffered over it. His slippery manner disturbed me: his shifting moods, his way of being friendly one minute and unpleasant the next, like some drunks who swear eternal affection for you but once the alcohol has worn off don't even remember who you are. I asked myself if ours was a true friendship. But what does that word actually ever mean? In order to know that, we would have to know the true nature of the self and its need to search for itself, recognize itself in and project itself onto others. But with Kuno it wasn't like that. I wanted to recognize myself in him, but instead I was continually forced to compare myself to him. Ours was a relationship with fluid boundaries and incomprehensible rules. When I felt as if I had come to the point of knowing every aspect of his personality, at the point where I believed I had been let in on the obscure rituals of his court, a last and inaccessible door suddenly appeared, and I could approach it only to eavesdrop. I had the distinct feeling that he wanted to use me. And yet I continued to play his game, and, deaf to all voices of reason, I fell ever more deeply under his sway. Without my being aware, our friendship, which had risen to its supreme fulfillment in an original burst of mutual genius, had already, and for some time, begun its descent, its countdown, or, to use a musical term, its *canone inverso*.

I REMEMBER a chilling episode, a "hunting accident" to which I felt myself an accomplice since Kuno forced me to swear not to tell anyone about it. What he did, an action I don't hesitate to call atrocious, was, in fact, a response to my refusal to relinquish my violin to him. He had asked an absurd thing of me and I had said no. And the evil act he then carried out in my presence was simply a warning: no one refused Kuno Blau without punishment.

But let me start at the beginning. One evening we had gone to the music room as usual. Kuno, however, didn't seem to have the least desire to play. He began to pull out his violins from the glass cases, and he wanted me to try playing them. At a certain point, his lips taut in a forced smile, he asked me to give him mine. He would give me another of equal value, he said, or he would pay me for it. I couldn't help showing him how unhappy his offer made me. For me, that violin was of inestimable worth. Could I ever trade or sell my head or my heart? Naturally, I refused. Seeing my face, Kuno tried to turn the whole thing into a joke. "You didn't actually believe that I was serious, did you?" But he was pale, too pale. My no had been for him an intolerable defeat. Nevertheless, at the time, I truly wanted to believe it had been a joke, even if one in bad taste.

A few days later Kuno convinced me to go shooting with him. I had never picked up a shotgun in my life, but he assured me that to fire a gun was the easiest thing in the world. In fact, he said, laughing, seeing as there was the possibility of war, I would do well to familiarize myself with firearms. Against my will but to make him happy, I agreed to carry on my shoulder the weight of a weapon I would certainly not use.

We left early and walked for a long time, accompanied by two hounds, a male and a female, which every once in a while disappeared into the brush, emerging anew from a place we never could have predicted. Their job was to round up a few wild animals and drive them in our direction. They ran back and forth looking at us unhappily, and their short barks seemed to scold us for our ineptitude. Now and again they were able to make a few birds extract themselves from the thicket and rise into flight, but most of the time they were too far away. The truth was that we weren't that interested in shooting. We spoke without lowering our voices and scared the game. But the subject of our conversation—immortality—was worth far more than a full game bag.

Kuno walked ahead of me down a narrow path while I listened to his lucid arguments. There is something extremely vulnerable about a person who, with his back to you, talks for a long time and never turns around. Something about what he is doing arouses a sort of compassion in you. You realize that he is, in fact, at your mercy. You can observe him without being seen, and you could strike him easily if you so desired, but at the same time this undefended position of his disarms you. And so it is with his words, his theories, his convictions—they too become disarming. The word "immortality" said by an old man, pronounced by the rheumy mouth of Mayor Klotz, sounded like a strident contradiction. How can a man who is already at the dusk of life talk about immortality? But uttered by a young man, barely more than an adolescent, at an age when he has just recently become aware of death and, at the same time, the perfection of life, a youth on the threshold beyond which everything relentlessly heads toward decay, from him that word assumed a powerful significance, it revealed an invincible will. But I was not won over by his reasoning. For me, only music had ever evoked immortality. Music was one of the many roads that led to knowledge, a road unknown to most men, but one that Kuno and I had been walking down for some time. Music existed before the world was created and could not be extinguished. And yet it was the most ephemeral of the arts, one that dissolves note after note. To dedicate one's life to the search for perfection in music was for me the only way to attempt to reach that ineffable state of immortality.

The path we were following was narrow and dangerous. Often, we had to walk along the edge of a crevasse or along a steep ravine from the bottom of which rose the thunderous roar of a stream. All of a sudden, Kuno stopped and signaled me to be quiet. Right then the dogs roused two quail from inside a bush. "Shoot," he ordered me. I tried to take aim in the way I imagined it was done, but I hesitated to pull the trigger. The two birds were having a difficult time taking off from among the webs of branches. The dogs moved in on them from one side, and on the other our guns pointed straight at them. Still I hesitated. Kuno fired and missed. When he fired again, his shotgun jammed. "Shoot!" he repeated angrily. I pulled the trigger with all my strength and felt a terrible blow to my collarbone. Kuno rejoiced: "You got it, you got it!" Without intending to, I hit the target, which often happens to beginners. Luck, unsolicited, had looked favorably upon me at exactly the time when I least wanted it to. I then saw the quail fall to the ground, its feathers circling among the branches. The two hounds headed toward it, disappearing into the underbrush. After a while the male emerged from the ferns with the catch between his teeth. Kuno ordered him several times to bring it to him, but the dog stayed where he was. The female circled around him excitedly, trying to steal the booty from him. In a definitive gesture, Kuno pointed toward the ground and commanded the dog one more time to drop the catch, but the hound began to growl and recoil as his master approached. I was overcome by unspeakable anguish; the forest seemed to be folding in on me, suffocating me, as I watched Kuno load his shotgun. I wanted to run away, but I only moved off a few paces. I heard him swear in a voice that was no longer his own. Never in my life, not even later during the war at the front, was the sound of a shooting bullet more terrible, nor the complaint in that brief yelp more bloodcurdling.

On the way home, neither of us uttered a word. Only when the castle came into sight did Kuno ask me to swear that I would say nothing to anyone. The episode was soon forgotten, or, rather, I felt the need to cancel it from my memory. I began by doubting my senses, and in the end I convinced myself that it had been a bad dream.

In order to keep a friendship we are capable of anything. When we surprise a friend in the most unseemly act, our judgment quickly grows dim, our indulgence blinds us, and the friendship emerges intact, grows deeper even, as if in order to develop to its greatest capacity, a friendship needed to feed off a friend's defects rather than his merits. In the end, what is friendship if not a tacit and reciprocal absolution con-

tinued over time? But that which was between Kuno
and me had come to a critical point. It had become
complicity.

Another "accident" occurred after the hunting one,
but this time I was directly involved. It happened one
evening while we were practicing the violin. The
Baron and Monsignor Ciliani, having perhaps taken a
break from their chess game, came down the corridor
and stopped in to listen to us. They sat against the wall
at the far end of the room in two armchairs. Kuno and
I were playing to the best of our abilities the unpublished scores, rendering with *arpeggios* and *fioriture*
the gallant spirit of the times in which they had been
written. Then, suddenly, I felt the Baron's eyes upon
me. He was staring as if something about me had
struck him. After a few minutes, I watched him rise
from his chair and remain standing for the rest of his
visit, leaning on his cane for support. When we had
finished playing, he came over to me, visibly curious,
and while I was putting down my violin along with the
bow Kuno had given me, he asked: "And where did
that come from?"

"Kuno," I said, a little taken aback. Luckily I had
only said "Kuno," and not "Kuno gave it to me,"
because Kuno, without looking at me, hurriedly
explained, "I lent it to him."

I was mortified. I remembered perfectly that Kuno had given it to me. And when I had hesitated to accept his gift, he had insisted that I take the bow and keep it as a memento of him, in case one day we were to fall out of touch. And when I, still unconvinced, had asked him what his parents would say, he told me he was at liberty to give away what belonged to him without having to ask anyone's permission.

The Baron, who seemed to have recovered from his shock, said to me, "Take good care of it," and then limped off dramatically, in a manner I had never seen before, almost as if he wanted to get away from me as quickly as possible.

Naturally, I said nothing, but that same evening I put the bow back in its place. I felt tricked. How was it possible that my friend had behaved in such a way? The following morning Kuno came to my room looking for me. He apologized, saying that yes, he had given me that bow but had forgotten to tell his father. Now, however, I could keep it. I, of course, no matter how much he insisted, wanted no more to do with it. Kuno's face was tense. I stood my ground. I saw that he could barely contain himself, his fists clenched, his body trembling. "As you wish," he said, lifting his arm and holding the bow as if it were a whip. For a moment, I thought he wanted to strike me in the face.

Instead, he struck the windowsill with such violence the bow broke in two.

"It would have been better if you had accepted my offer," he said to me and, turning on his heel, left the room.

PERHAPS COMMON SENSE should have persuaded me to leave the castle then and there. But something kept me at Hofstain. I stayed closed in my room, practicing. Only once in a while did I stop to listen if he too was playing, if music still united us. Never before had my life seemed so difficult to grasp. Even my memory of Sophie was crumbling. I was destroyed, without will. I passed entire afternoons sitting at the window in my room watching the light slowly fade across my walls. A month had already gone by since my arrival, and the season was coming to an end. Every day the shadows descended from the mountains more quickly. Often sudden storms rose up and the rain battered against the walls and windows with unusual violence. The dogs whined with terror. The rain swept across the rooftops covered with thin sheets of lead, channeled itself into a complicated network of gutters, and, in many resounding waterfalls, fell to the ground, which soon became flooded.

As usual, that night at the table two lit candelabras shone brightly, and even though it was still late summer, a fire blazed in the fireplace. The old Baroness had already retired for the evening. It was a Friday. Mayor Klotz, the doctor, and Monsignor Ciliani were once again holding forth on their favorite subject. It was a discussion that seemed never to end. Or, worse, that continuously started over from the beginning.

" 'Immortality' is a big word," said Mr. Klotz.

"Everything has a beginning," conceded Dr. Egony. "Once science has conquered all disease, life could last two, three, four hundred years. It would be the beginning of immortality."

"But prolonging the life of the body does not mean prolonging the life of the soul."

"What does that mean?" Egony always became irritated when the word "soul" was mentioned.

"For argument's sake, let's say science does eventually succeed in prolonging human life by two, three, or four hundred years. The question we must ask ourselves, which we cannot fail to ask ourselves, is this: The soul— "

"The soul, the soul," interrupted Egony.

"The psyche, if you prefer, or spirit, that which constitutes in our bodies self-knowledge. Let's say the mind—yes, the mind. The question, then, is: How will the mind be able to live during those extra years? What will the 'mental' value of a century be to a man who can live two, three, or four? We risk giving man's body the capacity to last three or four hundred years, while his mind doesn't know how to live even a minute more."

"I don't follow you."

"The future, for our minds, for our psyches, which conceive of a life expectancy of more or less seventy years, is seen as tomorrow, in a month, in a year, in five or six years. Our mind is not capable of imagining a future much greater than that. And the past, measured in centuries instead of years, would practically deprive us of the experience of growing up and growing old. Everything would be a mere repetition—yesterday or a century ago wouldn't make much difference. The past and the future, these two boundaries of consciousness, would become frighteningly close together, and we would lack real temporal perspective. In other words, what would two hundred, three hundred, four hundred years be without the consciousness of having lived them? For me, true immortality should not be the perpetuation of the body but rather the expansion of the mind. Immortality should be a continuum that begins at the origins of humanity and embraces the future. It would be a closed circle in which the past bonds with the present and the future. It would be an absolute unity. Then even a mere second of our lives would transform into the boldest theory of eternity that has ever been imagined."

"The limitless prolongation of the life of the body," intervened Monsignor Ciliani, "would have tremendous consequences. Man would have to carry with him indefinitely the unbearable weight of his sins."

"But he would also have plenty of time to repent," Dr. Egony retorted.

Ciliani made a vague gesture with his hand. "Sometimes a lifetime is insufficient to atone for a sin. But a life without end would be too much. No, certain things simply cannot be gotten rid of without death, without the gift of divine oblivion, the supreme gift, by which all of our guilt is relieved through His pity." Monsignor Ciliani sighed deeply. "The immortality of an individual would also become the immortality of his inabilities and weaknesses. A stupid man would always be stupid. A man lacking an ear for music"— and at this point Monsignor Ciliani turned toward me and Kuno and gave us a meaningful look—"would never acquire it, even if he lived for a million years.

What would be able to develop in him to excess would be wickedness, cruelty, insensitivity, all the vices that, like the thirst for power, know no limits. Hatred feeds on itself. And thus an abominable being would enrich himself during hundreds of years with ever new and abominable experiences."

The prelate became gravely silent, looked around him, coughed, then aligned his utensils on his plate.

THE TOLL of a pendulum wall clock reminded us that it was already nine o'clock. But that evening, instead of rising from the table as usual to move into the game room, the Baron began to speak. Most of the time he limited himself to listening, commenting on what was being said by nodding his head now and again. This time, however, he verbally asserted himself. Immortality, according to him, should be understood simply as continuity, as the memory of one's lineage. And as an example he used the old music Kuno and I had rediscovered. In the history of the Blau family, he said, there had been many talented musicians, and something of their abilities had surely remained alive and been passed on from generation to generation, culminating in the exceptional aptitude of his son.

The Baron's words humiliated me. I felt a rage

growing inside me. I saw the smallness of my past, like a door slammed behind me. I felt like a beggar forced to witness the grandiosity of immense wealth. The logs crackled in the fireplace; an icy air slipped into the room from the hall, disturbing the radiant glow from the candelabras. Again, that repugnant wound was reopened—my past, absence, the void, nothingness. Everything, then, was passed down; nothing was given. The past was like an enormous treasure chest one took things from during life's journey—a gem, a gold coin, a ring—things that could, however, be lost along the way. But if everything was passed down hereditarily, if everything came from that bottomless well, humanity's destiny, then, had to be in decline. If it were possible to go backwards in time, to return to our origins, leaping across the heads of our ancestors like rocks sticking up from a stream, at the end of this path each of us would find, necessarily, perfect beings. In the beginning, then, was the earth populated by gods who were full of every possible goodness, but who were condemned to dissipate it through their off-spring? If the form of a nose or the color of eyes reappeared in infinite variations, where did talent come from? Where did genius, imagination, the power to create come from? It was not possible for me to think that all of this was already contained in some distant relative, pure heredity of the flesh, and that nothing was added along the way as a gift of the spirit. This is what I was thinking as I listened to the Baron's words, but at the same time I wondered if I was justified in thinking this way. I was tormented by the suspicion that if one day I were able to discover my past, I would perhaps act in the same way as Kuno and his father, looking with recognition at my ancestors, at least for having given me the illusion that death is conquerable thanks to this perpetual passing down. Couldn't the fear of death be somewhat eluded by convincing yourself that you already existed before your birth, and that nothing was ever lost in the bloodlines? If, during the orbit of existence, it was excluded that every so often, as a result of joined bodies, a thunderbolt flashed sending a gift from heaven and not from plasma alone, one must then conclude that the bastard, the foundling, the nameless whose past would never be unveiled, was already a reject, one of the living dead.

Without being entirely aware of it, I was already saying these things. For how long had I been speaking? I, who during the past few days had hardly opened my mouth, was so stunned at how articulate, emphatic, and confident I sounded, I almost frightened myself. I listened to my voice become continuously louder. It was not possible, I was saying, that talent was only the sum of a lot of mediocrity spread here and there in the past. Talent did not come from that, not from a blood tie, but from a gift of the spirit. And becoming increasingly fired up, I concluded with these words: "A musician, as much as he might have taken from the past a predisposition or an appreciation for music, will not come to anything without this gift."

I realized immediately that I had gone too far. Kuno's father, surprised by my attack, used his linen napkin to clean the corners of his mouth several times and, embarrassed, mumbled: "Opinions . . . opinions . . . of course . . ." But the words remained in his throat, leaving everyone in thoughtful suspension.

And perhaps the dinner would have concluded in silence if it hadn't been for the words of another guest at the table.

"So, you think you have been given this gift? But how can you be so sure?"

The man who said these words with an insinuating tone had been a guest at the castle for a few days, but I hadn't spoken with him before then. That evening, he was seated rather far from me, on the same side, so in order to see him I had to lean forward, as he was doing at the moment. Besides the glow from his shaved head, he looked like a government functionary, with a paint-brush mustache, glasses, and a dark suit. His presence cast an ominous shadow.

"Well?"

I had no idea what to respond. I felt paralyzed by the stare that coldly assaulted me from behind thick spectacles.

"Come on," Kuno's mother intervened, "the boy surely has talent and has shown it." Then, turning toward her son: "Both boys have demonstrated that they have it." I saw with relief that the man with the shaved head desisted from his role as interrogator. Kuno, then, quickly arose from the table and left the dining room.

For the rest of the evening and the next day he didn't say a word to me. He only spoke to me a few days later, but his anger had not yet entirely disappeared. "How could you show such a lack of respect for my father? How could you behave in such a manner toward your host?"

"I was only expressing my opinion."

"Ah, really? Is that truly your opinion? Talent is a gift that only a few, like you, have, and all others are denied?"

"I said that talent is a gift and not something inherited. That's all."

"Right, of course," he said with a mocking smile. "From whom could you have inherited it? From your sausage seller of a father, perhaps?"

"He is my stepfather!" I yelled. "My father was . . . was . . ."

I became silent. I couldn't find my voice. My mind felt like a vast open space assailed by gusts of wind. For a moment everything became clear to me, but that which in an instant I had thought I understood was in another instant forgotten.

AFTER A FEW DAYS I decided to apologize to Kuno's father. I found him in his office. Perhaps it was only my impression, but the Baron, besides accepting my regret without showing the slightest resentment toward me, demonstrated on that occasion an interest in me that took me entirely by surprise. He wanted to know everything about me, about my family, about my passion for the violin, and I briefly recounted the story of my life. He seemed sincerely grieved over my mother's recent death, and when he took his leave of me not only had he pardoned me, but he advised me to trust in the gift of talent I had been given. This indirect reference to my unfortunate outburst of the other evening caused me to blush. Later, I also apologized to

Kuno. The meeting with the Baron, the interest he had taken in me and the generosity he showed me, made me ashamed of my lack of manners. And for a little while, everything returned to how it had been. At least it seemed that way.

A few days later a certain Hans Benda arrived at the castle. He was a musician and a friend of the family, an imposing man with gray hair, a gray beard, and a surly disposition. Besides being a pianist, Hans Benda was also an excellent composer. At lunch he told us that he had heard that two "young virtuosi" were staying at the castle, and that he had brought with him one of his compositions: a sonata in E minor for piano and two concertante violins, which he would love to play together with us. Placed before a new score, musicians act like children with a present—they want to unwrap it immediately in order to find out what it is. We begged him to let us begin practicing the sonata together that afternoon. After finishing our lunch, we gathered in the music room, where Benda tried out the Neumayer grand piano, then pulled out his score, handed us our parts, and Kuno and I began to play, reading the notes for the first time. It was a very beautiful piece, of which Benda was proud. He guided us with invaluable suggestions and with the passion of an orchestra conductor. *"Piano, pianissimo,"* he whispered, and his imposing figure seemed to diminish. Or: "*Appassionato,* here . . . at this point *con brio.* . . ." At the places of greatest force, he would raise his hand—if it was not needed on the keyboard—his palm upward, as if he were balancing upon it the small of a ballerina's back. Or, when he thought our playing was too loud for his personal conception of *pianissimo,* he would lower his hand ever closer to the ground, as if he were patting an invisible dog. It was a difficult piece, above all due to the fact that we couldn't allow ourselves to interpret it even minimally, seeing as the author was present and had a choleric temperament. Kuno had decided, as usual, to take the part of first violin, which was the more interesting, but which contained a few passages that were rather arduous. And he found himself in serious difficulty in the Adagio un poco mosso, which was by far the happiest movement of the whole sonata. Every time we repeated it, Hans Benda's heart seemed to break. We practiced it for a long time, but there was a point where Kuno was tripped up over and over again. Finally, Benda lost his patience. A break, he said, would do us good. Kuno, however, did not want to give up and insisted that we continue to practice. His face was red with annoyance, and his annoyance became anger when he messed up yet again.

It was then that I did something I never should have done, and to this day I regret. I couldn't even say if I did it out of friendship—what remained of it—out of a wish to help, or out of my own frustration and a pride too long repressed, out of a desire for revenge. While Kuno was once again attempting the insidious passage, I decided to show him how I would do it— playing the passage with diabolical ease, never even looking at the score.

"Bravo!" said Benda, upon hearing his music played correctly. "Excellent. Maybe it would be better if the two of you switched parts."

Kuno's face turned from red to livid. His violin and bow hung down on either side of him like two broken wings. He stared at the score, incredulous, as if he were staring into the face of a traitor.

"It would be better if we played again a little later," he said, almost in a whisper, and, turning as if to leave, all of a sudden he doubled over and collapsed onto the ground, trembling uncontrollably. Benda and I rushed over to try and help him, but Kuno, lying on the floor, continued to kick, his face stricken, his eyes rolled back into his head, and from his clenched mouth came a plume of saliva. We called for help. Dr. Egony succeeded in opening his jaws and stuck a finger in his mouth in order to unroll his tongue, which otherwise would have suffocated him. There was a boy from my village who often fell into these kinds of fits. I knew what it was and observed the scene in terror. Kuno's mother then put her hands on my shoulders and led me away. "It's nothing," she said. "It's nothing. He got too much sun, that's all it is."

Kuno was brought to his room and put into bed. The following day other doctors were called to his bedside. I saw them speak with Kuno's parents, who nodded gravely. I kept my distance. I would have liked to have seen him, but I wasn't allowed to. I felt guilty for what had happened and I wondered how he would act toward me now. Without him I didn't dare sit at the table, so even at night I stayed to myself. And no one seemed worried by my absence. From a distance, I watched the people around the dinner table as the candlelight created grotesque expressions upon their faces, and it all seemed entirely unreal.

THAT NIGHT I had a dream from which I awoke with a start. I dreamed that I was walking along a path in the open countryside. I was walking toward my father. He was, however, not as I had always imagined him, riding a bay horse, and he wasn't wearing a saber or a uniform. He was sitting on the edge of the path with his back to me. As I got closer, I realized, but without surprise, that he resembled Baron Blau. He was surrounded by a group of friends who were all talking, and their voices were so confused that I could understand nothing of what they were saying. I finally reached my father, and looking over his shoulder, I saw my violin resting on his knees.

At that moment, I woke up. My heart was beating fast. The ticking from the clock in the room echoed that of the pendulum clock hanging on the wall in the corridor outside my door. Otherwise, the silence was impenetrable. Even distant sounds like the call of a nocturnal bird or the bark of a dog seemed suspended, exterior, and did not scratch the profundity of the quiet. The images from that dream continued to roll around in my mind. I was not sure if it was a suspicion or a reminiscence, but something was certainly wanting to make itself known to me. It was the same sensation you feel sometimes when you hear a musical phrase in a downpour of water, a song in the ringing of bells, or, in the noisy confusion of a group of people, a chance word or two that attract one another and form into a complete sentence. I thought of a few days before, when the Baron was recalling the war with some of his former comrades-in-arms, and I heard them mention the name of the village where I was born. And now that sentence suddenly seemed to make sense. "Like that time," the Baron had said, "when our regiment was stationed in Nagyret. . . ."

At that moment something went off in me like a loosed spring. All of a sudden a whole series of fleeting clues solidified into a cast-iron conviction. It was like what happens with some watches that are believed to be broken and remain untouched for many years, but which one day astonishingly begin ticking again all by themselves. I sat up abruptly in bed and turned on the light. I felt both ecstatic and terrified. Never in my life had I experienced such an exciting confusion in my head. Mine was an idea that was both enormous and impossible. My existence shone, escaping every shadow, every mystery.

For hours my thoughts turned around in my head, one undermining the next. I wondered if it could be possible that my passion for music was only a means for destiny to enable me to discover my past. It all seemed a marvel to me: my violin had led me to my father's house. Now everything was clear: it wasn't the bow Kuno had given me that had attracted the Baron's attention, but my unmistakable instrument, the one he had left with my mother during the war, and that, after many years, had inexplicably found its way back to him.

I also, then, had a father and a lineage behind me, a place on a branch, even if it was the branch reserved for bastards. I, too, would be saved from oblivion and death. The Blau blood also ran in my veins, and Kuno was my brother. That explained the immediate attraction we had felt for each other and that I had wrongly attributed to a mutual passion for music. And that was why I thought I had seen myself in him.

I stayed awake the whole night, tormented by these thoughts. I didn't dare fall asleep for fear of losing them in my slumber. But the first light of dawn restored in me a more cautious sense of reality. Everything was clear, but nothing was certain. There was no truth to yell out, as I would have liked to do, to the four winds. An unwritten but strict code of honor imposed itself upon me. I had to resign myself to the renunciation of any claims, sealing everything inside myself as if it were the most terrible of all secrets. Only when spoken do things come alive. Silenced, even the most evident truths lose all right to existence. Was this perhaps what the Baron was trying to tell me with his reference to the gift I had been given? That I should content myself with suppositions and to keep quiet? At the same time, I realized, as per the rules, that the time had come for me to leave, to take myself far away, with the tacit promise never to return.

Nevertheless, when I went downstairs that morning, bright and early, as usual, I felt as if I were walking on ground that belonged to me. I observed anew the gallery of ancestors, searching for resemblances, and my imagination was so excited that I had no trouble finding them. I had an entirely new way of moving solemnly through the rooms, and I now regarded the servants fearlessly. Even to the manservant who was dragging his feet as he walked down the hall, I felt I had the right to give an order: that he prepare my things for my departure the following morning, as I said in a confident voice, and that he tell Baron Kuno that I desired to see him. The valet nodded, in a manner he had refined over the years, and went off. I waited, sitting on a couch. More than an hour went by. Finally, the valet reappeared at the far end of the corridor, coming toward me, but his pace was so slow I thought that the floor must be rolling in the opposite direction. When he finally reached me, he said: "Baron Kuno will receive you, but first he would like you to visit the rooms above." He handed me a key and, turning around, returned to his duties. I don't know how long I remained seated. Kuno was challenging me. In the end, I made my decision, and before the castle woke up, I went up the stairs toward the hidden rooms Kuno had pointed out to me when I first arrived, and unlocked the door.

I found myself in an enormous sitting room piled full of furniture, trunks, bolts of cloth, and the remains of what appeared to me to be the backdrop for a stage. With some difficulty, I made my way around all those obstacles. I was attracted by a curtain—hanging as if in a theater—of thick green velvet that divided the room in two. I went over to it and pulled back a corner, raising a cloud of dust.

I didn't see the picture right away. I had to take a few steps forward. It was leaning against the wall under a window, together with other oil paintings that had been gnawed on by mice. It was of the same dimensions as that pale outline I had noticed on the wall of my room above the chest of drawers. Had it been removed so that I would not see it? The painting was smaller than its frame suggested. The man in the portrait was holding something in his hand—a walking stick perhaps—which, due to the semidarkness, I couldn't make out. I went closer. It wasn't a walking stick but a roll of sheet music, and that which I had half expected to find was there at his feet—a violin, my violin, which the painter had reproduced down to the smallest detail, so that the head with that cruel and pained face was in the foreground.

I contemplated the painting for a long time in a sort of lucid swoon. Here was incontestable proof that all I had conjectured was true. I didn't know anymore if minutes or hours were passing. I didn't tire of looking. Then a noise behind me broke me out of my trance. It was the valet, who stood still, patiently waiting. How long had he been there? On his cheeks, shaven with extreme care, were intricate networks of tiny purple blood vessels. I saw he was smiling faintly. For a minute I thought it was a malicious smile, but then I noticed that his colorless eyes were filled with the light of infinite comprehension, that which we imagine to be possessed only by one who has reached great wisdom. He had come up there to tell me that Baron Kuno was ready to see me. Etiquette dictated that he accompany me, and it was a very slow journey. Finally, I crossed the threshold of my brother's room.

Kuno was in bed with his back leaning against pillows. His face was still pale, but there wasn't a trace of suffering in his features.

"You've come to say good-bye before leaving? Sit down." But I stayed where I was at the foot of the bed.

"Before you go, you should know something," he

said. "My father once played the violin and was so passionate for it that he carried his instrument everywhere with him on all his trips. There was in particular one violin which he would never be separated from, almost as if it were a talisman. When he left for the war, he took it with him to the front, where it was stolen. It is for this reason that I asked you to give it to me, because it doesn't belong to you. I don't know how you came to possess it, but whoever gave it to you, perhaps even your father, was a scoundrel."

JENÖ VARGA staggered up from his chair. He was exhausted. He drank the last drops of Obstler from the bottom of the empty bottle and put it back in his pocket. He seemed drained of life, a mannequin dressed in dirty clothes. I looked around me. Night was full-blown. Vienna finally lay sleeping in a silence rippled only by the song of nightingales.

The man adjusted his cape around his shoulders, placed his derby hat on his head, picked up his violin case, and said good-bye to me: "I wish you a good evening, sir." He yawned, turned his back to me, and took off across the courtyard. I followed him.

"One minute—just one minute!" I said, before I realized I was yelling. From the other side of the street, a passerby (the last of the night walkers or the first of the early birds?) turned and stared at us.

At the sound of my voice the violinist stopped, tucked in his shirt, and then began walking again.

"Hold on a minute!"

I came up beside him. "Will you allow me to accompany you? Your story is not over. And Sophie? Did you see her again? What became of Sophie?"

He stopped as if he had been hit by some unforgivable oversight. We then continued walking for a while before finally he began to speak again:

After fleeing from Hofstain as if I were a thief, I returned to my apartment in Vienna, and for the first time in my life I saw everything as hopelessly bleak. During that time, I thought only of death, and everything around me seemed to suggest it. If I leaned out my dormer window, the courtyard looked to me like a ravaged cemetery, with tombstones strewn across the ground and sniffling stone angels soaked by the rain. For days and days, I hardly ever touched my violin. It seemed to me that its voice had lost all splendor. I had the suspicion that the humidity permeating that attic had caused irreparable damage to it. The truth was that I couldn't find any comfort in it anymore. That which I had always feared had happened—music had abandoned me, and I had lost all power to call it back. I tried to play, to practice as I had always done, but every stroke was like an empty room with distorted acoustics. And when I put the violin back in its case, it lay there, with its lionlike face, resembling a chimera arranged in its coffin.

I began to ask myself if there was still room in this world for music. I noticed alarming indications that there wasn't. One day, while I was going up the stairs, I had to stop and wait because four exuberant moving men were carrying down a piano held by straps, and with every step they swore, cursing music and all those who dedicated themselves to it. The baritone had wound up bankrupt and in jail and his only asset was being seized. I would never again hear him sing his passionate arias. And a few days later, across the street from our building, hanging very visibly in the window of the fruit-and-vegetable market, I saw a sign that said: WE DON T GIVE CREDIT TO MUSICIANS. Was it possible? This sign in the capital of music? But by now the only music in Vienna was military marches—on the street, on the radio, you heard nothing but the roll of drums and the blare of brass. In such a martial din, I wondered what role my violin could possibly have—that of cheering up the troops during their leisure time? I realized I should be playing folk songs in barracks or bivouacs. Or I myself should take up a gun.

For the first time, I understood the world had changed, that it was deprived of its light. I could not stand to be around people. I did not recognize myself in them, I did not share their ideals, I did not understand them. As I walked in the streets and squares, I was ripped apart by panic. The people had become a crowd, an indistinguishable throng, that funneled through the rigidly laid-out streets of the city, pushed on by its own bewilderment. There was a terrifying urge to gather together. No one wanted to be alone with his own conscience. The silence of churches and houses was abandoned, as was the tempered heat of candles and table lamps. Missals and books were closed in order to go out and mingle with the others, to hear the shrieks that announced an impending catastrophe. The most common spectacle to be seen was the political rally, the debate in the square. On street corners, persons above suspicion would mount overturned crates and begin to harangue the crowd, before police on horseback charged in and dispersed the gathering. I had never seen such crowds in all my life. I had never seen in the people's eyes a light so joyful and so tragic at the same time. Not even for the Messiah, perhaps, had there been such expectation.

AS FOR SOPHIE, I had by then forgotten her. It was as if I had left a part of me at Hofstain and now whatever was left, that part which wandered lost through the streets of Vienna, was a being without ideals. I was convinced that I would never play again, that my dedication to music had been extinguished forever, and along with it the image of Sophie and all dreams of love and perfection. One day very soon, I would knock on the door of my stepfather's company and say: "Here I am!" And that decision would have brought me all sorts of advantages. I would wear a dark suit with a gold chain and a gold watch. I would travel, and maybe during one of my trips I would see her—oh, not as I had always imagined, no, I would see her from afar, our paths would cross in some hotel somewhere, and I would ask for the room above hers, so I could lie down on the ground and listen with my ear pressed against the floor.

ONE DAY while I was roaming the streets of the city, I was drawn to a poster that had recently been put up on a wooden fence. I went nearer to it and read some striking news: Sophie Hirschbaum was to perform in concert in Vienna. Life seemed to flow back into me. For a moment I had the illusion that the world, my world, was not entirely over.

So after five years I saw her again. I paid a sum way beyond my means for a seat in the orchestra. I wondered if she would be able to see me, and if she would recognize me. I was by now a man, and if she did remember me, the picture she would have retained was that of a boy.

When she appeared she was extremely elegant, in a long dress of black silk pulled in at the waist with a scarlet ribbon. She seemed to be a mirage produced by the crossed beams of spotlights, cleverly poised in momentary equilibrium, ready to disappear at the least sign of a shadow. Once again I saw her severe expression, her readiness for a challenge. I had the impression that she was looking straight at me, but probably everyone in the orchestra felt as I did. Then, all of a sudden I was gripped by panic. My heart began to beat very fast. I believed Sophie was in danger, that all of us were in danger, and that we had to do something. Everything seemed on the point of falling apart from one minute to the next. Was it possible, I wondered, that no one among those present was aware of what was about to happen, that on their faces there wasn't the least sign of worry? Neither the musicians nor the conductor, Joachim Boehme, showed the smallest concern. How could they, I asked myself, stay peacefully in their seats waiting to begin, with their instruments in their hands and their eyes turned toward the audience, without feeling that which was weighing heavily in the atmosphere? All of them, Sophie first and foremost, were going to play music, upsetting every rule of communal daily life, and would be able to do so with incredible insouciance. They were calmly seated in front of their scores, thick with streaks of black dots, waiting to obey, in full harmony, a gesture that was both a command and a subjugation.

Sophie went over to the first violin in order to determine her pitch. She leaned toward him, as if they were telling each other secrets, then suddenly lifted her head and looked as if she had just seen with perfect clarity all that the future held. She nodded to the conductor, who began without pause the allegro of the first movement of Mendelssohn's Concerto for Violin and Orchestra. And with the first notes, that sensation of an impending threat became stronger in me. I was tempted to stand up and yell: "Silence! Can't you see what is happening?" It was as if from far away, I could hear once again that cacophony that I had heard for two hours every day, for two hundred and forty days a year, for five consecutive years at the Collegium Musicum—the cacophony of an approaching hurricane making its way through the creaking tree trunks, and in its fury toppling them, breaking branches, and upsetting flocks of clamoring birds trying to escape by the thousands. The world was heading toward dissolution and no one seemed to be aware of it. The musicians, the conductor, even the soloist—my adored Sophie—persisted in closing their eyes and offering order, rhythm, harmony. They should stop it, I told myself, and remain silent, listening for where the danger was coming from.

It was during the second movement, in the middle of the andante, that this sensation took actual form somewhere behind me in something that resembled the distant sound of a chorus humming, a murmuring that slowly grew louder until even those around me heard it. It came from the back of the room, and some in the audience began to turn around. Finally, someone tried to quiet the troublemakers, but to no avail. Saying "Ssshhh!" and acting indignant were not enough. The murmur became ever louder and was accompanied by stamping feet, so that it became an intolerable roar, and the concert, after a signal from the conductor, was interrupted. The lights were raised and words became insults, which in turn became punches, and a brawl broke out in the balcony. Soon the police barged in and removed the hooligans from the theater. The lights were turned down once again, though the beam of a flashlight continued to wave about in the balcony. The turmoil, however, was not over. Voices could still be heard in the foyer, and from the street came the sound of firecrackers and chanting of incomprehensible slogans.

The concert began again and was played in its entirety. But at the end of it, in addition to the applause, whistles came from the rows of seats in the rear. The whistling spread and soon drowned out the applause. People began to leave. Sophie Hirschbaum, the great violinist whom the public had always worshiped, often obligating her to perform endless encores, would not even have taken a bow before making her exit if Boehme had not taken her by the hand and insisted on bringing her before a group of fans (I foremost among them) who continued to applaud. By now I was extremely close to the stage, and I looked into the face that for all these years had filled me with great emotion—and still did.

The crowd dispersed. It seemed that everyone was following the fire safety rules tacked to the wall of my stepfather's offices in Vienna. In the case of danger, abandon the building "promptly but without panick-ing." Taking advantage of the general confusion, I reached the stage, and within a few minutes I was in the midst of musicians gathered around their dressing rooms. I called out for Sophie and someone directed me to a corridor. At the far end of it, I found a room that was not only empty but looked as if it had been abandoned in a great hurry. I followed an arrow on the wall pointing to the performers' exit, and was just in time to see her headed toward the open door of a car, surrounded by a gesticulating crowd, from whom Boehme, still in his tuxedo, was trying to protect her by making a shield of his body, his arms raised over her like the wings of a hen. Finally the car left, its horn honking.

I went outside and mixed in among the people who were still waving their arms in the direction of the departed automobile. These people who had waited by the performers' exit were certainly not fans. I walked among them listening, trying to understand the reason for their rage. It was an anonymous crowd, attracted, in its stupidity, to a sign of power, to something that promised to satisfy its repressed base instincts, a crowd that had come, in a sort of sleepwalker's stupor, to take part in a lynching, a public execution. It was a crowd that rumbled, and came together in order to see what

was going on, a bobbing crowd that was moving forward, "promptly but without panicking," toward
perdition, turning their backs on salvation, blindly
aiming toward the place of their own annihilation.

I extracted myself from those bodies and went to
the front of the theater. Scraps of paper were scattered
over the steps leading up to the entrance. Posters and
notices had been ripped from the walls and covered
with offensive graffiti and swastikas.

A FEW DAYS later I heard someone knocking on my
door. I ran to open it. A man with a shaved head, a
fashionable mustache, thick-lensed glasses, and an
insinuating voice stood before me. I recognized him
immediately. He was the one who had asked me, that
evening at Hofstain, what made me so sure I had talent. My assessment had been correct. He was a government functionary, a police official. He was inquiring
about my violin. He showed me a document, dated
1698, confirming its acquisition by Johann Blau. And
now Kuno Blau requested the restitution of the instrument. Did I want to go through the ordeal of a trial?
Have my father's memory dragged through the mud?
And be judged myself as the receiver of stolen goods?
The man with the shaved head spoke with unexpected

kindness. He was sorry about the unpleasant situation that had arisen, and he understood my dismay. But there was no alternative. It was not right for me to want to keep a stolen violin, knowing that it was not rightfully mine. I said nothing. I looked for a last time at my violin before closing its case. The man with the shaved head came over to me and took it. He headed toward the door. I didn't move. My compliancy seemed to make him feel pity for me, and before leaving he gave me a reassuring smile. "Courage, son—the world is full of good violins, and when also joined with talent . . ." But he didn't know that for me everything was now lost.

A few months later the troops of the Third Reich invaded Austria without firing a shot; in fact, they were received with open arms. In March of 1939, I enlisted. In September, the war broke out. I was sent to the western front and then to the Russian front. And I had the good fortune to return home alive. But to what home? I knew that my stepfather had been an army supplier, that his factory had been gravely damaged by bombs, and that he had tenaciously begun rebuilding. But in 1946, he was killed in an automobile accident. Of Kuno Blau, I knew nothing. As for Sophie, having survived the camp at Treblinka, she was defeated by tuberculosis in a Swiss sanitarium.

And I followed her. Just as I had always sworn to do in life, I did the same in death.

I DIDN'T UNDERSTAND what Varga meant by these last words. In that moment, however, my only thought was not to let him out of my sight. He had significantly picked up his pace, and I was having difficulty keeping up with him.

"Will I see you again?" I asked him.

"I don't believe we will see each other again. I am going home, but if you would really like to, you can come visit me. Everybody knows me down there."

I followed him for a little while longer, but finally I let him get too far ahead. He turned around one last time. "Remember," he shouted, "that musicians are Cain's progeny—Genesis 4:21." Having said this, he began almost to run, his cloak flying up behind him, and from one moment to the next I expected to see him leap into the air and fly up, far above the rooftops, to the sky, which had by now cleared. I continued to follow him, although ever more slowly, until at a crossroads I lost sight of him.

I returned to the hotel at dawn's first light. I didn't go to bed, but took up a pen and paper and began to write down what I could remember. I felt that I had the elements of a story. I worked for the whole day and well into the night, when finally I collapsed from exhaustion. The next morning, I read my frantically written notes, but everything was already fading in my mind, and many things didn't seem to make sense.

I stayed in Vienna another few days and began to do research in newspaper libraries and music schools. I succeeded in speaking with a number of musicians who had been educated during the thirties, but no one could tell me anything about an institute called the Collegium Musicum; nor, though at the time a rigorous discipline was enforced in conservatories, had anyone heard of a school that practiced such rigid study methods. And I was unable to find out anything about a violinist named Sophie Hirschbaum. Evidently, my narrator had changed the names of places and people. I wandered the city in hopes of meeting up with him again. For some days, I went up and down the street where I had seen him for the first time, but without any results. I searched in all the cheap hotels, in every social assistance center, in every pious house of charity, but no one could tell me anything about an itinerant musician named Jenö Varga.

I was ready to leave Vienna. In all likelihood, the man I had met several days before in Grinzing was something of a prevaricator. And yet, in the mad lucidity of his story, in the heartfelt tone of his confession, there had been something genuine. I thought of writing, perhaps not a novel, but a kind of diary. I had filled a notebook with what I had seen and heard in those two unforeseeable evenings. Nevertheless, I was not convinced. Leaving Vienna, I felt as if I were quitting a game that was not yet over.

His last words returned to my thoughts. In speaking of Sophie, he had said that he had followed her, just as he had sworn he would. Followed her where, I asked myself—into death? Certainly not physical death. Perhaps Varga meant another kind of death, a death of aspirations, a spiritual death. And the violin, "that violin," where had he got it from? Hadn't the police official with the shaved head taken it from him? Hadn't it been returned to the music room at Hofstain? Sometimes, I withered with the doubt that Varga's story was some sort of slightly sinister practical joke. I thought about his last words over and over again. And then all of a sudden I understood that before he left, he had given me a clue.

"Come visit me," he had said. "Everyone knows me down there." Down there, down there . . . He certainly didn't mean to allude to Hell, I told myself, but surely the town in which he was born—what was it called? Nagyret? It couldn't be too far from Vienna, either. So the following day I rented a car and found myself on the road to Hungary. I consulted a map and found two towns with that name. But the Nagyret that interested me, if I remembered well, was near the border between Slovenia and Austria. It was not easy to find. When I reached the village, resembling so many others scattered across the Magyar plain, it was almost evening. Clusters of low houses, ranging in color from ocher yellow to iron gray, were right on top of each other along the main street. Many secondary streets shot off of it, leading nowhere but to the open countryside. It was a town that, if it hadn't been for the laundry hanging out to dry in the tiny backyards, I would have thought abandoned. The only building that was distinguishable from the houses was a small church that had been painted magenta. I parked the car in the shade of an elm and walked around the town. Only after a little while did I begin to detect signs of life: a curtain pulled back, a voice or two, a little old lady dressed in black who made the sign of the cross as I passed . . . until finally I arrived at what must have been the town's one gathering place. I had passed it earlier in the car but hadn't noticed it. It was no different than the other buildings except for a dirty green curtain that hung over the entrance, and for the few signs advertising beer labels that were in the windows.

It was a tavern—the right place, it seemed to me, to ask for information. I went inside, trying to maintain a certain nonchalance, and said hello in German to two customers and the bartender, whose faces didn't change expression even by a wrinkle. The place was bare, with a dirt floor, and from the ceiling hung a fly strip that had long since been completely covered. The bartender answered me in Hungarian. He was evidently asking me what I wanted to drink. On the large wooden bar sat an earthenware demijohn. A plastic tube with a valve attached to it stuck out of its neck. Since it seemed to be the only drink in the house, I indicated that I would have a glass of it. The bartender cleaned the bar top with a cloth, removed a heavy glass mug from a rack hanging on the wall behind him, and filled it with wine. I sat down at a table near the door. The wine, if it even was that, was terrible. After a little while, feeling that I was being watched, I tried to approach the other customers. I asked if any of them knew a certain Jenö Varga. I received no response. None of them seemed to understand my words. I continued nevertheless to speak, because the sound of my voice was at least reassuring to me. I pronounced Jenö Varga's name many times, and I even mimed the gestures of a violinist. But the three men remained impassive. The bartender continued to wash bottles in a basin of soapy water and then place them upside-down on a dish rack.

Suddenly, one of the two customers got up from his table and left the tavern. I stayed seated for a little while longer, sipping at that acidic wine, but when I got up to pay, the bartender indicated that I should stay. I didn't have to wait for long. The curtain covering the entrance was pulled aside; the customer from earlier reappeared and gestured to me to come outside. Behind him was an old priest, a man more than seventy, with dark skin; and speaking in perfect German, he told me he was the parish priest. I felt greatly relieved. I left some money on the table and walked with the priest toward the church.

"You came for Jenö?" he asked me, after a while. "Poor boy, and a great talent. Here everyone still remembers him."

I didn't quite grasp the meaning of his words. We reached the little church, but the priest continued along a path that went around it, leading me toward a little cemetery enclosed by a stone wall. I followed him through the gate, among the graves, until he stopped before a gravestone surrounded by rampantly growing saxifrage. I read, carved into the stone, the name of Jenö Varga and the dates of his birth and death: 1919–1947.

"This isn't the person I'm looking for," I told the priest. "I spoke with Jenö Varga only a few days ago in Vienna. This must be someone with the same name."

"A few days ago?" The priest seemed disturbed. "And what did he talk to you about?"

I briefly told him the story.

The priest shook his head, perplexed. "It would seem that you had actually spoken with Jenö," he said. "Except I myself buried him nearly forty years ago. And over there, come see, is the grave of his mother, who died in childbirth when she was thirty-seven."

"No, no," I said firmly. And the priest, who was already on his way down a small path, turned around. Then, with some hesitation, he asked me: "Are you sure you saw—?" I interrupted him. "I am not sure of anything anymore."

When we reached the cemetery gate, the priest invited me to his house. But I couldn't wait to get out of there. I told him that I had an urgent meeting in Vienna, said good-bye, and started walking toward my car. After a few steps, I still heard him talking. Without stopping, I turned my head slightly toward him and heard him say: "Sometimes the dead find the strangest ways of communicating with the living."

On the way back, near Sollenau, perhaps overcome by fatigue, I fell asleep at the wheel and went off the road. When I awoke, I was in the hospital with both arms broken and a serious contusion to the head. I had been unconscious for two days. When I was released, I found my bags with all my personal effects except for the notebook containing my notes, which had been lying on the seat next to me. It had been lost in the accident. But had I really written those notes? Had I really met Jenö Varga? Had I really seen his tomb at Nagyret? I didn't dare look into it further. I preferred to think, after the accident, that reality and dream had come together in such a way that it was no longer possible to distinguish between them.

Some time has passed since that strange encounter at the Dorchester in London. The man, whose name I could not remember even if I lived another hundred years, left as he had come, taking with him an unfinished story, an enigma never to be resolved. I made no mention of the psychiatric institute. When asked where the violin had come from, I lied, telling him that the owner had wished to remain anonymous. Perhaps I should have told him, put him on the right track, but I couldn't have done so without revealing myself. And that, after so many years of silence, was unthinkable.

IN THE REGION surrounding Innsbruck the snow begins to fall harder. The young driver I hired upon my arrival from London slows the car, thank goodness. The windshield is covered with snow except for the *demi-lunette* openings thanks to the vigorous work of the old windshield wipers. Before us, we can just make out an overturned tractor-trailer stretched across the road, and men in yellow raincoats wave their flashlights at us, indicating a detour.

As we leave the highway, it seems that under the shelter of the fir trees the snowstorm suddenly abates. We continue along a narrow and winding road. It is nearly dark, and the headlights have difficulty cutting through the swarming snow. When we come to a fork in the road, once again I have to knock on the glass. "Hofstain is the other way!" I yell in a shrill voice I myself don't recognize. Why do they make me yell at my age? There is nothing worse than an irascible old man. The driver, with an indifferent shrug, backs up the small distance needed to then take the right direction. My new driver is not disrespectful; no, it's not that: his is simply the arrogance of youth. Often our eyes meet in the rearview mirror and I realize I am being observed. Sometimes, I am obliged to move over to the far left of the backseat in order to avoid his stare. The black window reflects my image, but in the place of gleaming sky-blue eyes, I see a hairless, bony bird of prey, the wrinkled face of a nonagenarian. Snow has begun to accumulate on the road, but even after many years in the tropical climate of Colombia, my faithful Daimler rides as if on velvet, without the smallest sign of skidding.

When we arrive at the castle, it is already evening. Luckily, the two housekeepers come out to meet us immediately. Who knows how long they have been waiting for us? My only contact with this married couple has been by letter. They are much older than I expected, having been informed of their ages only when they were hired, how long ago I cannot say. He is small and thin. She is taller than he by at least a hand and seems to be in control of the situation. With consummate experience, she gives the necessary instructions to her husband concerning the suitcases, and informs the driver of where he will be staying in the servants' quarters. Old, I thought, though much younger than I. But their agedness is subdued, while mine is insolent; they are resigned to it, I am still challenged by it. I am the old lord of the castle for whom all the lights and all the fireplaces of Hofstain have been lit, and for whom dinner has already been prepared and placed at the head of a long empty table.

In the end, I eat only a bite or two, accompanied

by a glass of Burgundy, so as not to cause offense to such an exquisite cook. I then dismiss the two servants, asking them to leave me alone. What is left for an old man like me? The wealth I had acquired while in search of the philosophers' stone—the allure of gold irresistible to the alchemist—has allowed me over the years to regain all that my family had lost, including, finally, the violin of this story. Yet what remains is the immaterial past, that overflowing abyss. And every so often, a memory alights on its edge, fluttering like a butterfly in the breeze.

I leave the table, the dinner almost entirely untouched, and I go into the library. I sit on the small couch in front of the large portrait of Margarete, and my heart begins to make itself felt. If old age brings blessings, they are not wisdom or experience, but the rediscovered memories of our youth. The opaline skin of her hand resting on the keyboard of the harpsichord appears absolutely clear to me. I see again her smile as she plays French airs. And while she performs Rameau's "*Le rappel des oiseaux,*" in the vast garden the light is already fading, and the flocks of birds rush together from far and near. The tree branches are quickly crowded and a loud chorus arises, which is suddenly silenced when night falls. It is dark. I light the candles so that she can see the score. She smiles at me. Perhaps she shares my thoughts. In the light from the flame of the candelabra, her face seems to be looking out from a painting by La Tour.

Never have I desired her more! As if gathered up into a sweet hallucination, I seem to assume her face, I have suddenly become another being; for a moment I have the privilege of contemplating her, in the same way that I perceive myself, from the interior. I squeeze my eyes shut, I shiver with surprise, I smile. And her face covers over mine to perfection, I am inside of her and she fits me like a sumptuous suit of clothing. She is skin and I am epithelium; she is expression and I emotion. But she is still my brother's wife.

And I didn't know how to accept that. I fled to the other end of the world, swearing that I would not return as long as she was alive. But I never imagined that the letter I sent to my mother in which I told her of my decision and the motive for my departure would arrive so late, and due to a strange case of mistaken identity, an unknown suicide, buried in my place in the family cemetery. The grave is now empty. I learned of the night in which the stranger's body was secretly exhumed and taken to rest in other sacred ground. But my mother could not withstand such emotion. And she was marked by it for the rest of her days.

It seems funny to me that now, among the historic

tombstones of all the members of the Blau dynasty, there lies a stone that already has my name on it. Actually, one is missing. But soon he too will join us. I still carry in my pocket the letter I received not long ago from the Mariahilf Institute of Vienna, where my nephew spent his last tormented years, and I cannot resist the temptation of reading it once more.

Honorable Baron Gustav Blau,

I am responding with some delay to your request. For many years, I have had under my care at the Mariahilf Institute a patient by the name of Kuno Blau. I have only recently become aware that he is a direct relative of yours. The subject suffered from schizophrenia of a fairly typical kind, with delusions of omnipotence (he frequently suggested he was immortal), and over time he began to manifest with increasing frequency the signs of a double personality. Finally he reached a state of being permanently split into two personalities, each well defined: The first was submissive, characterized by asthenia, having difficulty with deambulation, aphasia, and loss of memory.

The second, the dominant part, was plethoric, exhibited logorrhea, had strong musical aptitude, and called himself Jenö. The violin seemed to be the only thing they had in common, the link between the otherwise distinct personalities, even if it was approached in very different ways. In the case of the first, named Kuno, he regarded the violin with a total sense of ownership which at times became a fetishistic attachment. Instead, for the one who responded to the name Jenö, the violin was a true means of expression (the subject revealed himself to be a violinist of great talent). In the final months, this second personality ended up dominating, and eventually entirely eclipsed, the first, in an irreversible delusion that lasted until his death, by heart attack, on December 18, 1985. Unable to locate any living relative, all of his personal effects were sold in order to cover, at least in part, his confinement, and the corpse was interred at the Baumgarten Cemetery, whose administrators you should contact with regard to all the necessary arrangements for the body's transferral.

I followed this particular case with great interest, and if you would like to know more about it, I would suggest you read the next issue of the journal Die Neue Psychiatrie, *in which, respecting anonymity, it is described in extensive detail.*